COSCOM
ENTERTAINMENT

ALSO BY A.P. FUCHS

BLOOD OF MY WORLD TRILOGY

DISCOVERY OF DEATH
MEMORIES OF DEATH
LIFE OF DEATH

UNDEAD WORLD TRILOGY

BLOOD OF THE DEAD
POSSESSION OF THE DEAD
REDEMPTION OF THE DEAD

THE AXIOM-MAN™ SAGA
(LISTED IN READING ORDER)

AXIOM-MAN or
AXIOM-MAN: TENTH YEAR ANNIVERSARY
SPECIAL EDITION
EPISODE NO. 0: FIRST NIGHT OUT
DOORWAY OF DARKNESS
EPISODE NO. 1: THE DEAD LAND
CITY OF RUIN
EPISODE NO. 2: UNDERGROUND CRUSADE
OUTLAW
EPISODE NO. 3: RUMBLINGS
FROZEN STORM (SIDE ADVENTURE)
SCARLET SYNERGY (SIDE ADVENTURE)
THE SUMMONING
EPISODE NO. 4: TRANSFORMATIONS
NEW DAWN
OF MAGIC AND MEN (COMIC BOOK)

MECH APOCALYPSE

MECH APOCALYPSE

The Canister X Transmission: Year Two
The Canister X Transmission: Year Three
The Canister X Transmission: Year Four
The Canister X Transmission: The Long Year Five
The Canister X Transmission: The Very Long Year Six
The Canister X Transmission: Year Seven

Poetry

The Hand I've Been Dealt
Haunted Melodies and Other Dark Poems
Still About A Girl
Caught in Black Headlights

WWW.CANISTERX.COM

EPISODE No. 4

BATTLE OF POWER TRILOGY BOOK TWO

AXIOM-MAN™

TRANSFORMATIONS

by

A.P. FUCHS

COSCOM ENTERAINMENT

WINNIPEG

ISBN 978-1-83436-007-2

Published by Coscom Entertainment

Text set in Garamond
Printed and bound in the USA

Cover art by Kevin Phillips
Cover design by A.P. Fuchs

This installment is for those who know what it's like to be stuck in the dark and having to fight your way out.

You're a hero.

BATTLE OF POWER TRILOGY BOOK TWO

AXIOM-MAN™
TRANSFORMATIONS

PROLOGUE

THERE WAS NO light. There was no sound.

There was nothing.

Axiom-man tried to let his body's sense of touch assess his surroundings. A breeze. A smell. Spatial awareness and the sense you're drifting by something or something just brushed past you.

There was nothing around him, so far as he could tell. He moved weak arms through the air, paddling through it as if trying to swim. He moved his legs in a slow bicycle motion, thinking maybe his feet would find purchase on something beneath him—but there was nothing.

Open your eyes. The fatigue was so great that forcing his eyes open took more effort than trying to speed through the air. He only caught a glimpse then had to close them again. He played the image in his mind, freeze frame: blackness with wisps of red cloud floating and moving a good ways from him.

Axiom-man tipped forward and a bright light pierced his eyelids, forcing him to squeeze his eyes shut tighter. It didn't help. He tried to move a hand to his face to help shield his eyes, but his limbs were so weak he couldn't raise them past a few inches. He gathered himself deep within and put all energy toward opening his eyes.

When he did, a force like an all-engulfing set of hands grabbed him and pulled him through a tunnel of twisting colors and light, rainbows of reds and oranges and yellows and blues—sometimes all lined up together in its respective spectrum—blasts of black then white streaks.

Axiom-man sped through the tunnel, speed picking up and not by his own effort.

He wanted to yell out from the momentum encompassing his body, propelling him forward at jet-like speed, but he couldn't form the words.

Lights.

Rainbows.

Colors.

Black.

White.

A gray hand reached for his shoulder.

CHAPTER ONE

SOMETHING MILDLY FIRM was beneath him, kind of like a hospital mattress but much thinner. Axiom-man tried to get a feel for what was beyond the mattress but couldn't place it. He wanted to open his eyes to see where he was, but trying to open them was like trying to lift a train—he couldn't do it. Just the black of closed eyelids and what was probably black surroundings.

"We need to wake him," said a voice.

"No," said another, female. The authority in her tone made it clear she was the one in charge.

"He has to get up."

"He has to come around on his own. I will not interfere with his waking. There are factors at play you do not understand."

Axiom-man expected a reply but the other voice fell silent.

Another voice spoke, male and familiar. "I may have chosen wrong."

———

Skin touched Axiom-man's forehead. All was still dark but the realization he was without his mask hit him hard. He did a body check and couldn't sense his uniform either. He could be mistaken; he was so tired. He tried again to open his eyes, thought he felt his eyelids move a little, but then had to keep them closed. A rush of heaviness clouded his mind and muffled voices spoke somewhere beyond the fog.

Only one word stood out: "Over."

———

An icy chill ran along Axiom-man's body. The cool air was so vivid he was certain he was naked and whatever ice just passed over him froze a layer of sweat along his skin.

Uniform. Mask. He started to drift off again, unable to help himself. *Somebody knows who I am.*

———

"How long has it been," a voice said.

"It doesn't matter here," the female replied. "This has to happen naturally."

"Or else?"

"We lose him."

———

The dreams were periods of darkness and utter silence. Axiom-man didn't know how long he had been out. He knew some duration of time had passed due to being in that black place for an indiscernible period then coming around to where he knew he was awake but couldn't move or see.

During those periods of darkness, there were no voices. No feeling throughout his body. Just a consciousness existing in a black void. He thought he might panic, being stuck like this, but instead he felt nothing. Not even his own heartbeat.

I'm dead, he thought. *No. If I was dead, I wouldn't be here. I'd be . . . nowhere.* A thought struck him so hard it caused a tingle in his brain. *Am I inside the black cloud? The Doorway of Darkness? Am I a prisoner? Did . . . what was his name? Did he kill me or trap me or . . . ?*

What was his name!

The urgency of the thought melted and then a longing for someone filled him.

Someone.

Special.

Important.

Gone.

———

It took intense focus and a whole lot of strength, but Axiom-man managed to open his eyes about a quarter of the way. He was on his back. Above him . . . some sort of ceiling of aged wood, rough—maybe. Too blurry.

His eyes dropped closed. Axiom-man tried to force them open but couldn't.

But at least he had been able to open them.

Wherever he was, it was dead quiet. He strained his ears for any indication of sound or movement or . . . or . . . those voices from earlier, one familiar. But there was no one.

Insides heavy, his body sank further into the backing beneath him.

Black and silent again.

———

I need to get up, Axiom-man thought. He concentrated and was able to open his eyes around halfway. Too much blur distorted the room, and he second-guessed himself on the wooden ceiling. He tried to look at it but couldn't make out anything amidst the shadows.

If you're a hostage, you need to get out. It was then he realized that while unconscious, his powers had *shifted* off. *Float. Rise. Straighten. Move.* Whoever had him could not keep him. Anything untoward would jeopardize . . . jeopardize . . . . His head swooned and he couldn't land the thought.

Axiom-man drew inward, focusing on his body, his mind, his heart. *Shift. Change. You can do this. Push.*

But there was nothing there.

His powers were gone.

———

If only he could see the room better. If only there was some light, anything to give a clue as to where he was. Axiom-man tried *shifting* again, the hope being to illuminate his eyes as he usually did when stuck in the dark.

The powers would not come. He couldn't even feel the deep internal option to *shift.* Though his head was fuzzy and it took forceful effort to form coherent thought, he recognized how he felt.

Normal.

Just like he did before the messenger first visited him and gave him his powers. He had to admit, the sensation of having no abilities was both familiar and comforting, yet foreign and discomforting. He had known his powers so long. Had known walking around with the ability to rise above any occasion, ultra abilities on standby if needed. Knew he could act like a nerdy goofball and get away with it because he was secretly something more underneath. There had always been an inherent confidence that came with that and, right now, that was gone too.

Axiom-man's heart ached. His thoughts drifted to Valerie and the sting of shame punched his heart when he acknowledged he solely thought of himself right now instead of what happened to her.

He couldn't help it.

One thought and moment at a time. It was all his brain could handle. Everything about who he was and is he compartmentalized, only able to access one item at a time, forgetting all of the rest.

What was wrong with him? Where was he? Who did those voices belong to?

But Valerie. She was gone. Gone-gone. Forever. Dead and murdered by a psychopath in a black mask.

"I'm going to kill him." He could only mouth the words but he felt better after making the effort. *I will kill him, figure out some way to raise him, then kill him again. I will do it over and over until it is no longer possible.* He took in a breath through his nose. The room was dank and smelled of rotting wood, though, from what he could remember, the wooden ceiling didn't show any signs of rot. *What is this place? Oh Valerie, what have I done? What . . . who . . . where . . . where'd you go? Why go? I'm so lost.*

The door opened.

Chapter Two

Axiom-man shut his eyes and hoped he wouldn't drift off so as to miss what might be said.

"I know you're awake," the female voice said.

Don't give her an inch. She has the upper hand right now. Don't speak. Listen . . . then act.

"Breathing changes when someone is awake than when they're asleep, but I know you already know that. Everybody does. I'm just letting you know that despite your effort right now to alter your breathing to make it seem as if you're sleeping will not work with me."

She had him there. He had tried faking. *Idiot.*

"Your name is Gabriel Garrison. You are also known as Axiom-man." When she spoke next, she was right beside him. *How did I not hear her come near?* He could only assume his ears were still not hearing correctly. "The name Axiom-man is no longer yours."

"What?" The word barely came out but he hoped she heard him.

"Wearing that mantle under your watch just cost your planet."

My . . . planet?

"That name will not be spoken again. Do you understand, Gabriel?"

No, I don't understand. I came up with that name. You can't take it from me. I am Axiom-man. "How dare you?" The words were mouthed again. Try as he might, he couldn't summon enough strength and air to speak them out loud. He wished she'd heard him.

"As it stands right now, Gabriel, I can dare to do whatever I want."

Was she a lip reader?

"Who—?"

No reply. He waited. Still no reply.

Gabriel forced his eyes partly open, and though his vision was blurred and his peripherals were unreliable, he was pretty sure he was alone.

"Who are you?" It was a whisper, but at least it was sound.

———

Gabriel must have drifted off. Listening. The exertion of attempting to speak. The thinking.

The dark.

Something wasn't right. There was something around him.

Before, he couldn't move. Now . . . slowly . . . he managed to shove his arm along what felt like wood. It took a moment, but he realized he was no longer on the mattress but laying on something hard. He moved his other arm, dragging it farther from his body along the hard surface. Not an inch of movement later and his forearm butted up against a wooden wall. He checked the other side. Same thing. As much as he wanted to, he couldn't lift his limbs. He wanted to see if anything was above him to confirm his suspicion but he didn't have to. A muffled voice somewhere above him confirmed it.

He was in a box. A wooden box.

A coffin.

I'm not dead! "Help!" He swore he heard himself scream the word but knew nothing came out of his mouth.

"What if he doesn't come out?" someone said.

"He will," came the female voice.

"What if he doesn't want to?"

Another voice came. Gabriel knew that voice but couldn't apply a name to it. "He will."

———

Redsaw's red energy beams fired a hole through Axiom-man's chest. He looked down at his ribs and a cauterized, ragged wound about the size of a baseball ran right from the front of him straight clean through the back.

Then the dark returned and Gabriel awoke, still confined.

What is this? Hell? Wasn't I a good person? Good people don't go to Hell. But something told him that wasn't true, that Hell was the destination of everybody unless they made a particular choice. What that choice was, he didn't know.

"Help!" Sound came, but not loud, yet a giant leap in amplification compared to before. At least he heard himself say the word.

Silence.

Dark.

The coffin, if that's what it was.

"He doesn't need someone to stand guard," came a muffled voice. "He's not going anywhere."

"And you know this how?" The female again.

The other person didn't respond, and Gabriel got the feeling the other person didn't know *how* to respond, but there seemed to be a connection between the two people.

That rooftop. That explosion. The Doorway of Darkness.

Valerie!

Tears pooled and leaked out of his eyes, running out the corners and down his temples. The water poured. He tried to let himself cry it out but the concern over where he was seemed to stifle the release. All he could do was let the sharp sting of loss and failure strike his heart with guilt and shame as the tears ran from his eyes, and Valerie's visage danced in the dark.

"Valerie." Gabriel thought maybe there would be a reaction to her name from somewhere on the other side of the coffin's lid, but there was nothing. Were those people even still there?

"Redsaw," he said.

The tears kept coming.

————

The thirst hit him hard. Gabriel didn't know why it hadn't before. He must have been inside this coffin for a couple of days now, never mind the time laying on that hard mattress plus all the exertion to stop Redsaw and save Valerie.

The image of Redsaw slicing her throat with a blade of red energy flashed across his mind and immediately the tears pooled and leaked out. He tried to reach up to his face to touch them but couldn't get his hand more than a couple of inches off the hard surface they lay upon. Gabriel tried licking the tears with his tongue, hoping maybe one trickled to a place he could reach it, anything wet to soothe the thirst. His tongue didn't reach and panic set in. A person could only go so long without water. Food—that was easier. The body would turn to itself for energy, the fat first then the muscle, but water, that was what was required for most bodily functions and right now he had none.

Gabriel parted parched lips and said, "I'm thirsty." He waited a moment. "Anybody?"

Oh please, let someone be there. His captors seemed to have a plan for him. Seemed to ensure he was kept alive. Maybe they gave him some water while he was unconscious? Just squirts from a small syringe to the back of this throat and some instinctive swallowing. He didn't have to go to the bathroom so if indeed he was fed liquid, it wasn't enough to fill his bladder.

"Is anybody there? I need . . . I need help. Someone?"

Silence.

Again.

Either there were people on the other side of the coffin lid and were purposefully quiet, or no one was there at all. Whoever had him, had him for a reason. He just didn't understand what, and there wasn't even a *why* because his powers were gone. What use was he to them other than maybe a source of information?

You need to get out of here. Strength is slowly returning but until I can use my arms or legs, I'm stuck. His back ached from laying on it for so long against the hard wooden surface. To sit up and stretch the lower back would be glorious, but that wasn't an option right now.

He spoke to the coffin lid. "Are you nailed shut?" he said into the darkness above.

"What if he doesn't come out?" An echo of the voice from earlier. Earlier *when*, Gabriel didn't know. His internal clock was off due to drifting in and out of consciousness plus whatever lengths of time he was asleep. He could have been in this coffin for a mere day or two, or he could have been in here for much longer. He didn't know and didn't care.

He needed to drink.

"He has to." The female from earlier.

Gabriel's mind was a little clearer now so he considered the statements. He was to come out of this box . . . or die within. There seemed to be a tinge of confidence to the tone of the woman who spoke, "He has to." It was almost as if she knew he could do it but was merely waiting.

She might have to wait a long time, Gabriel thought. *Or maybe I can surprise her?*

Getting out of the coffin, if managed, was all fine and good, but then the issue was what he would do once out and what he would do if those two people were in the room when he did. As of now, he could barely move.

He didn't know how long he should wait until he could try escaping the dark.

CHAPTER THREE

VALERIE. THERE. IN between the columns, her skin bubbling as the heat began to consume her. She looked at him, her eyes glazed. "Gabriel . . . help." It looked like she tried to reach her arm toward him, extend her hand, a desperate plea for assistance before she . . . before she . . .

Gabriel was shocked back to the dark of his tomb. He couldn't get to her fast enough. Couldn't get there *before* Redsaw had put her between those bright red columns. Couldn't get there in time to stop the madman from reopening . . . . Redsaw had reopened the Doorway of Darkness and the city of Winnipeg was unprepared.

This was all part of his plan, Gabriel thought. *The chaos, the riots, the looting. Battle Bruiser. Lady Fire. Bleaken. And some person in a gray outfit.* He even wondered if Gunn was somehow a part of it, him having made some sort of deal with Redsaw to deliver Axiom-man right into his hands.

The people on the other side of the coffin lid hadn't visited him in a while. Were they in on it, too? Were they his captors or guards or played some other sort of role that would keep him contained.

Gabriel let out a primitive shout and growled. He listened for any response, some sort of reaction to his cry.

Whatever was beyond the lid was quiet.

He wondered if the absence of his powers had an effect on his body. Even after all this time, he still didn't understand how his body communicated with his powers or if his powers and parts of his body were somehow intertwined. The removal of his abilities had messed with his eyes or his muscles, sapping them of strength and maybe that was why he had such a hard time moving.

His back ached with a series of cramps from being stuck laying down for so long. He'd lost track of time a long time ago.

The air in here was thick and stale, its thickness coming from all the carbon dioxide he'd been exhaling and the containment of his own body heat in such a small space. If he had any moisture in him, if they had still been giving him enough water to stay alive even while he was asleep, it was entirely used up by his body and there wasn't enough for sweat. Just claustrophobic heat that told your insides to do a twist.

Water.

He needed water.

He needed—

Water. Unless his perception of time was completely out of sync with reality, there was no way he should be alive. Not after this long. The hunger pangs had vanished some time back, so the discomfort of a growling stomach was no longer an issue. But the water was. He was somehow being fed enough to keep him going. Slowly, he lifted one arm enough to rise above his belly and fall onto his other arm. He felt up and down its length, checking for an intravenous of some kind.

There was none.

He checked the other arm. Same thing. He did a quick body scan, paying careful attention to sensations in and on his skin, thinking maybe he'd feel something stuck in his leg. Pushing himself, he reached down and felt his legs as best he could. He couldn't find anything.

His thoughts paused and all was blank for a moment. Gabriel feared he might be falling unconscious again. The moment passed and coherent thoughts returned. If he was fed water, that would mean one of two things: The lid wasn't locked down by nails or any binding system to seal it shut. To give him water would require removal of the lid so they could position him in such a way as to administer it. That wasn't to say something wasn't on top of the lid once they sealed it again, but the possibility it was moveable gave him a little boost.

And the other option. That one might be the chink in the armor. They could be running a tube down to him *through* the lid to give him what he needed. He'd have no way to tell due to the dark.

That lid sat above him. Closed.

And he wasn't strong enough to lift his hands and press against it.

———

They say madness comes on slowly. Gabriel disagreed. If he had to spend any more time locked up here in the dark, he'd surely lose it. After everything that's happened, after the torture and unknowns, after losing . . . her . . . . He could see why some people snapped or were crippled because of something terrible that happened.

His heart pounded with anger and a swell of energy built up within him, desperately trying to find an outlet lest the rage consume him.

He focused all his concentration and effort to his arms.

Come on. Lift them. Nothing is pinning them down. Nothing is tying them down. You need to get up.

He grimaced then howled again, low and guttural.

"Come on!" he shouted. "Lift!"

He gathered all his strength and put the power into his arms. *Just an inch. No. Two inches. Three. Four. Push off this stupid wooden—*his arms began to rise.

———

It had been a futile effort. He managed to brush the inside of the coffin lid with the backside of his palms before his arms fell back to his side. All strength had run out of his front deltoids from the effort.

Why am I so weak? he thought. *No food. Hardly any water. Bad air.* His eyes widened a little. *The air!* He'd been in here long enough there would be no doubt he'd have carbon dioxide poisoning by now and would have suffocated a long time ago. Air was getting in. Barely, but enough to keep him going. Air getting in meant a crack in the wall, never mind how they were giving him water.

It was impossible to discern in the dark where the opening might be or if he was like a bug in a jar with holes in the lid. Either way, if indeed the lid was the access point for air, its structural integrity was compromised even if just by a little. Granted, the air hole could be on the sides or even somewhere along the bottom beneath him if this coffin was elevated in some way.

"Enough. You can't stay here," he whispered. At least he had the strength to speak a little. Finally. *Think. Whoever was on the other side said I had to get out of here. I don't remember the tone but I don't recall it being malicious. Granted, that could all be an act to get me out and then kill me. If these guys work for Redsaw, I'm as good as dead anyway. Can't do much without my powers. At least, not right now.* "Gabriel, you're doing this no matter what, no matter if it hurts, no matter if it seems impossible. You are getting out." What he'd do once out, he didn't know, especially if he encountered the people those two voices belonged to. But at least he'd be out. *Or they'll just beat the tar out of you and throw you back in here. If they do* . . . . It didn't matter. The effort had to be made. Powers or not . . . powers or not . . . he was still Axiom-man. *It doesn't matter what those people said. It doesn't matter if they know who I am. I'm not going to die in here. If I rise, and if I die, then at least I go out trying to stop that madman from destroying the world.*

The world.

The gravity of that thought sunk in. This wasn't about the city anymore. It wasn't even about himself. With the Doorway of Darkness open, there was no telling what might come out of it. It had only been open for a short time that night at the MTS Centre, and that short time was enough to cause all sorts of problems for the city. And for those it touched, including himself. If the new Doorway was open right now or even had been open longer than the first time, Winnipeg, himself, society—that was only part of the picture. Gabriel knew if Redsaw kept it open and drew power from it, the world would eventually fall. Everyone from every tongue and nation would be affected and, he was certain, would die if they did not comply with Redsaw's demands.

The sad part is Axiom-man could have been anybody. I learned that and it hurt. I was chosen because I was the last in line over generations who still had the ability to receive the powers. Had I been born different or if my folks produced someone else in my stead, that person would have received the powers. His heart ached, but it only made him angry. Chance or not, *he* was the one given the responsibility to use his powers for good. *He* was the one who, right here, right now, had to make the choice to finish the battle and end the war between him and Redsaw.

He just had to get out of this coffin.

"I'm not doing this anymore," he said, his words audible and firm. "I'm not doing this!"

Tapping into sheer rage, he forced his arms up, growled, roared, directed every ounce of strength he had into his arms and shoulders and placed his palms against the coffin lid. *Don't think. Just push the f—*Gabriel pressed hard against the lid, using his anger and rage as strength. He prayed to God that adrenaline would surge through his body so he could do this. *Push.* "Push!" With a shriek, he gave it all he had.

The lid lifted a mere centimeter at the pressing point.

"I am Axiom-man!"

"No, you are not." A voice. His head was so full of anger, he didn't know if it was the woman or the other one. Regardless, he wasn't listening to them.

"Shut up!"

He pressed harder, guiding the lid over to the right, moving it slightly, the wood heavy but not heavy enough to be cemented in place.

His arms burned from the exertion. His shoulders cried out for him to drop his arms and cut them a break. Gabriel wasn't having it. If he was going to die, he was going to do it on his terms in an all-out effort to get the hell out of this coffin.

With one last roar that sucked the air out of his lungs, he pressed with all he had and got the lid open enough where there was a space of about a foot to squeeze through.

The next problem was lifting himself out.

———

Gabriel couldn't remember how he managed to elevate himself slightly upright at an angle. All he recalled was squeezing his eyes shut with every effort. The closer he got to the coffin's lid, the more cool, fresh air filled his lungs and the stuffiness began to fade. His chest jerked when a small but hard cough escaped but his focus was on his hands. His fingers trembled as he gripped the edge of the coffin. The room beyond was pitch black and silent. There was no way to tell if he was alone or not. But it didn't matter. He couldn't wait. He didn't know if he'd have the strength to try to remove the coffin lid again.

It felt like all his adrenaline had already been spent, the rage and anger inside already beginning to subside as if the emotions themselves were too taxing on his body.

Grip and lean forward. Grip and lean forward. Grip and . . . . He leaned forward, the edge of the coffin digging into his chest and putting pressure on his lungs. Gaining air was near impossible and the little sips he could take barely helped with the situation. "Over," he breathed, the word barely a defeated whisper.

He rocked slightly backward then forward, backward then forward, some sort of momentum to . . . . He tumbled over the edge of the coffin, his body half hanging out. His palms touched the cement floor and, judging by the height, the coffin itself was floor-level. At least he wouldn't fall far.

Gabriel tried to drag himself out slowly by walking his palms along the floor in the hope he'd eventually pull the rest of his body with him.

There wasn't enough room. He needed more of an opening in the lid to get his legs out, but if he attempted to reach back and adjust it, most likely he'd collapse in an awkward position between the lid and the rest of the coffin and essentially get himself stuck.

He slowed his breathing and took in air through his nose. It helped fill his lungs a little less, giving him a bit more flexibility but also made them pound for more air.

Gabriel's elbows collapsed and his face smacked the floor. The awful sensation of water going up his nose spiked hard from the impact along with a slam to the bone of his brow. Tears pooling, he squeezed the moisture out and, slowly—it must have taken over a minute—pulled his palms right back against the coffin's side, bracing himself. He paused, gathered what little strength he had left, then put everything he had into pressing the heel of his hands against the box. At first, nothing happened, and the pressing made his arms burn and tremble. He fought. He pushed.

He gave it all he had and fell over onto his side as his legs loosened from their confines and left most of him hanging out of the coffin and lying on the floor. He used his arms to drag his body along the cold cement, each drag and pull agony on his muscles. To hell with them. This had to be done.

With a final growl, he got himself out and flopped to the floor, gasping for breath, his muscles burning and aching. The cool air and cold floor sent bizarrely relieving shivers through his body. Each breath of new air invigorated him though he could barely move.

Time passed. The dark remained silent. He may or may not have fallen asleep from the effort. All he knew was one moment he was on his side, the next more face down. Doing a push up to get up wasn't happening. He tried getting his elbows under him. It took a while, but once he did, he took a few minutes to rest and swallowed cold air in a dry mouth.

One leg. Just one. *Move it. Just . . . move it.* His legs wouldn't budge.

He started to weep when he realized he had to wait.

———

On his elbows, the cement floor pressing against the bones, Gabriel had his face on his forearms. He raised his head a little and focused on his right leg. "Come on." Slowly, he pulled it up so the knee was bent. Catching his breath, he said, "Okay, other one." He drew up his left so he was frog-legged against the floor. This was a bad idea. His pelvis and groin was tugged and pulled from the position. Concentrating as best he could through a foggy mind, Gabriel, smidge by smidge, pulled his legs inward, trying to get his knees under him. When his knees were close enough to his body, he braced himself for what was to come.

Don't lose momentum. Don't lose focus. Get the hell up. Get up, Gabriel! He lifted his torso just enough to get his knees under him . . . barely. He could scarcely breathe. It was like putting in an hour sprinting on a treadmill then being asked to do an hour more. Everything was rubber. This was not how it was supposed to work. The hero always came out on top, and here he was limited and, even trapped, by his own body.

"Arrhhhh." The sound was almost inhuman as he righted himself and sat upon his knees. Coughing, gasping for air, the effort made his head spin. All he could do was focus on an imagined point in the dark so as to, hopefully, not fall unconscious and collapse. If he focused on that point and kept his awareness there, it might stave off passing out and allow him to do what needed to be done. Except, there was no strength in his legs. He moved his arm through the air, bumped it against the coffin. Not wanting to lose the moment, he pushed against it. It scooted along the floor then stopped as if catching on something. Gabriel listened for breathing and any sound that might indicate someone had stopped the coffin from moving.

He heard nothing.

He pushed on it, his mind adrift in a sea of instinct for survival.

Gabriel fell back, his arm against the coffin stopping him from falling all the way. He dragged his legs until . . . he wasn't sure. He just knew he wasn't directly on his knees anymore. Pins and needles filled his legs. Just like anybody, he knew standing on legs that had fallen asleep was impossible.

Try. At least . . . try. He wanted to sleep so bad. Wanted to give into the dark and into the quiet. It would feel so good to rest, to let the muscles recharge as best as able, to have a chance to—his feet were under him.

Crap. I'm stuck. He wanted to stand, to make the effort, but he couldn't engage his thighs to help with the lift.

"Come on," he breathed. "Let's go, Gabe. Push." *You got this far. Don't waste it. Don't let him win. He can't. He's stolen everything. He's got to . . . go to . . .*

"Arrggghhhhhh." Gabriel stood very slowly. The moment he acknowledged he was upright, green stars clouded his vision and buzzing filled his ears. His legs gave way.

Someone's hands caught him under his arms.

CHAPTER FOUR

GABRIEL CALLED IT the wall. It was brick red, and he only knew this because of the dim lighting barely covering the area around him.

The color of blood.

The color of Redsaw.

A week of Redsaw. This wall. Though he couldn't be sure a full seven days was accurate, Gabriel had been against this wall learning to stand. Food and water slid in from the shadows into the tiny, dim-but-illuminated area. The food was always a healthy balance of meat, vegetables, and a bit of starch. He could breathe out here. Full breaths. Each one inhaled since coming out of the coffin serving as a salve against whatever toxicity had settled in his lungs from being inside it. The food was hard to stomach at first. His stomach had shrunk from not eating inside the box. He didn't even finish his first meal and simply did the best he could. Chewing and lifting the food to his mouth demanded tremendous effort. He slept. He ate. He tried to keep track of time. If it wasn't for being so weak, he would have taken a chance with the surrounding darkness to see where he was.

But not without the wall. Slatted wood ran horizontally, a tiny gap between the boards to give the tips of his fingers some purchase, the aim clearly for him to try and use the wall as a crude ladder to help him get to, and stay on, his feet. He learned early on in his efforts that, as he slowly climbed, the tips of his fingers numb from the pressure, he had to keep himself as close to the wall as possible to maintain center of mass. The day he was able to rise about forty degrees was a momentous occasion. He did his best to hold the position for as long as possible, to force his muscles to work and come back stronger next time. But each effort always led to a sweat-laden collapse, gasping for breath.

Gabriel's powers leaving him must have wrecked his body something fierce. Or it might have been the battle with Redsaw. It might have been all the fights leading up to it. One giant culminative, calculated effect to rob him of who he was.

Who he *had*.

Valerie.

Now, sitting with legs splayed out, back against the wall, the tears came and Gabriel placed his face in his hands.

I've failed everybody. The messenger. Valerie. The city. Even myself. My family never knew so I guess they can't be disappointed. He sighed deeply. *I'm so tired. I can't do this anymore.* He glanced up at the wall. Its top, which was only about six feet up, seemed like a skyscraper at the moment.

You can fly over that no problem, he thought. *As if. Not right now. Maybe not ever again.*

———

A plate of cobbled-together food slid near him. A piece of chicken, cooked but clearly stale, and a half-eaten tomato. He brought the chicken to his lips and slowly chewed, barely blinking, staring into the dark. The chicken was tough and dry from sitting out somewhere, tepid and plain. Juice dripped down his bearded chin, mixing with the hair as he finished the remainder of the tomato.

He wondered if all the red was on purpose. If this was Redsaw's way of always reminding him he lost. The red wall. The black shadows. The red tomato. The black inside the coffin.

You already feel him crowding in on you. You feel the pressure against your body, the air itself so thick with defeat and sadness, it's weighing you down. "Let it," he whispered. *Then what? Die? Why all the effort to stand then?* He didn't know who he was talking to in his thoughts. Probably just himself talking to himself because his body and brain were tired of trying, giving up, trying, giving up—all it wanted was a choice. *Live or die.* He glanced up again at the wall . . . and dug his fingers in.

————

Each pull upward was agony on his finger muscles and pounded through the tops of his hands, the tendons taught and strained. Each board was about six inches wide. His arms were strong enough now that he could lift them up. They weren't strong enough to lift himself entirely. But still, he pressed down on the very tips of his fingers as hard as he could as he got his feet under him. He reached up, took hold of the next board . . . and pulled while pressing down with his legs, digging his cold bare feet into the cement floor.

"Uuupppp," he groaned. His thighs burned from the exertion, and he did his best to use the pain as fuel to push harder.

He reached another board and dug in.

Grunting, he slowly rose an inch.

Just get the weight of your ass upright to straighten. Overcome the hurdle. Get over the hump.

He pushed with his legs and pulled with everything he had against the boards, shoulders fatigued and almost out of gas.

He started pounding out the breaths, each exhale like a bull grunting at its target. "Get. The. F—" With a guttural scream, he forced himself up then fell forward against the wall, sweating and panting, expecting his rubbery legs to give way at any moment and to tumble to the floor.

He leaned his wet forehead against the wall, its sawdust smell almost pleasant against the stench of not showering since who knew when.

Gabriel kept as much of his weight against the wall as he could, anything to help keep him vertical. He hadn't stood since first coming out of the coffin. His head swooned and his lungs burned from the effort.

"Ah," he breathed out. "Ah." Each exhausted exhale came with a sound.

The wall.

The red.

The surrounding dark.

He had to get out.

He wanted to glance over his shoulder to see how far he might have to travel into the shadows to find something to indicate where he was. *No. The view from up here is the same as down there.* He searched the dark anyway just to be certain.

Black.

From the other side of the wall, the female spoke: "Welcome, Gabriel Garrison."

"What? Who?"

He caught sight of her in his peripheral but knew a full head turn would cost him his balance and he'd fall at her feet.

From what he could tell, she was a little taller than him and had dark hair. Her face was ablur and, with most of his view taken up by the wall, he didn't know what she was wearing, if she was armed, if she was a threat.

There probably is, he thought. No one would treat him like this unless they wanted to drag out his torment and defeat at the hands of someone so vile, so evil—so powerful.

"You will remain like that until I say otherwise," she said.

Remain like this? He could barely keep his legs under him and already they were beginning to falter. He had to adjust to keep upright. "What . . . who . . . ?"

"I'm of no consequence at the moment." Beside her, a dark gray blur materialized. "Watch him," she said. "If he tries to leave, ensure he doesn't succeed."

Gabriel didn't hear a response or even see movement that might indicate a nod. The woman was gone when he peeked against his peripheral again. He took a moment, tried to relax, tried to calm down and save his strength to keep standing. He was in no condition to fight let alone move. *Just ride it out. Only chance. Only option.* "I . . . I've seen you," he said.

The gray figure didn't say anything. Just kept an eye on him.

"You're working . . . for a madman." He coughed. "You can't . . . you can't help him. Please. Let me . . . I need you to help me stop him."

Silence.

"I beg you."

The figure stepped behind him and two firm hands gripped his shoulders. Next thing he knew, the figure pushed and tugged against his arms, adjusted his footing and nudged his legs for better stabilization.

The figure had made standing easier.

"Why . . . ?"

TRANSFORMATIONS

The figure never made a sound.

———

Gabriel had been permitted to sleep on the ground for what seemed like a uniform amount of time before the figure in gray made him climb the wall again, get his feet under him, and made him stand for the entirety of his waking hours. As the days wore on, and as his legs rested while he slept, he slowly got stronger and standing became easier. The soles and heels of his feet ached from the constant weight upon them, but it was better than being inside the coffin. Once he was strong enough, he knew, he'd figure out a way to make a break for it and get out of here. After that, he would figure out how to stop these two from helping Redsaw any further.

When fed, he couldn't use the wall for the stability needed to build up the muscle. Gabriel had to concentrate hard to maintain footing and balance while also holding his dish and bringing food to his mouth. Like always, each meal was balanced and, he started to notice, high in protein. He wasn't through and through familiar with the body and nutrition but he did know the protein was meant to strengthen his muscles.

To make his point, he dropped his plate on the ground once done. It clunked down on the cement, wobbled for a moment, then settled. The figure in gray merely stepped up to it and, with one boot, kicked it aside, sliding it into the dark.

"What's your name?" he asked the figure.

No response. The figure didn't even cross its arms as if stating defiance.

"You have never spoken a word. Are you forbidden? Is it some kind of sick instruction from that woman to try to intimidate me?"

Nothing. The person in gray remained completely stoic.

"I've played enough games in all this. I'm not playing yours," Gabriel said. *But, obviously, you have something planned. Fattening me up for the kill? Get me strong enough so I can go through torture without passing out?* He had considered not playing the game. Not eating. Not even taking deep breaths to ensure lots of oxygen got into him and playing its part in his recovery. Yet if he didn't, any chance of survival or escape would be impossible and all would be lost to Redsaw. He just wanted to know what was within or beyond the dark. A door? Some sort of passage? How could he outrun the figure in gray who had its eye on him day and night? Did this person ever sleep?

The figure stepped up to him, their mask keeping any facial expression hidden. Gabriel considered taking a swing but he was still too weak.

The figure put a hand on his shoulder, squeezed firmly, and gave his foot a kick. His heel skidded a few inches across the floor . . . and standing was easier. The figure looked down at his foot then back at him. All Gabriel could do was nod. The figure had made his footing assured. It finally sunk in it was trying to teach him balance.

So Gabriel waited and stood and waited more.

———

Gabriel lay on his side, back against the wall. He hadn't slept, only pretended to. The figure remained motionless, sometimes shuffling its feet a few inches to the left, then again later to the right, but it never left its general spot. Gabriel was always under the watchful eye of a person who did not seem to need to sleep.

He couldn't stay here. He hated the waiting and how long it was taking for his body to recover. And even when he did recover, what then? A one-man army without powers against two people who seemed to know what they were doing or did a darn good job acting like it? If these two were indeed assigned by Redsaw, then it was a surety that whoever these two were, they were not hired goons but people with the ability to stop him should he try to escape. And the person in gray was no slouch. Gabriel had seen them move, and even if what he saw was all they could do, right now, it was more than enough to take him out.

Gabriel had no choice but to be patient.

———

There was only one way, one shot, so Gabriel took advantage of every opportunity to heal. He slept, he ate everything given to him, he breathed deep, and made sure he had as much water as he was allowed.

After digestion, there was a means to relieve himself on the other side of the wall, a simple bucket with a tight lid. It was embarrassing and humiliating, especially with the gray figure there, though it did give him the privacy he needed to do what he had to do.

Gabriel shuffled his feet along the floor, his legs getting sturdier by the day, strength returning to his limbs. He went to his spot by the wall and stood.

The woman appeared. "A vast improvement," she said. "Are you sure you don't have your powers?"

What? Of course he was sure. If he had them, he would have used them to get out of here by now.

"What does he want you to do with me?" Gabriel asked.

The woman gave a knowing grin. "*He?* He wants you strong. Truly strong. Then . . . he can see what you can really do."

What was she talking about? This didn't make any sense. He'd fought Redsaw before. Redsaw knew full well what he could do which was why he was in this situation now. Did Redsaw want him healthy enough so he could drag him in front of the people and beat him senseless, show the city their "champion" was a mere man and had fallen?

"You can't bring me to him. You have to help me," Gabriel said though he knew his words were met with deaf ears.

"We will bring you to him and we will help you."

"That's not what I meant."

She came closer, her movement fluid. The woman didn't walk like any woman he knew. She had a grace about her and body language that didn't betray any feeling or thought.

Gabriel and her locked eyes and he noticed how richly emerald green hers were. Her hair was jet black and her womanly form, though rightly proportioned and beautiful, appeared firm and strong. Who was she? A spy? Maybe this wasn't Redsaw? Maybe this was a foreign superpower, even minor power, that somehow got hold of him. And these two were somehow involved and he was doomed and—

"Gabriel," she said.

He snapped out of his racing thoughts and slowed his breathing to calm his racing heart.

"Breathe," she said gently.

He didn't know if compliance or defiance was the best choice right now. If only he knew more, if only there was some clue as to where he was. If only he could figure out these two people and . . . then what? Fight them?

Gabriel lashed out his fist at the woman, the reaction primal and completely instinctual. He didn't realize what he did until his fist missed and hit nothing but air. The woman wasn't even in front of him. There was only . . . darkness.

And something firm beneath him. He glanced to the side and saw the wall. Not only had he missed, he had somehow been put to the ground without feeling the impact.

The woman stood there while the gray figure moved close to him. Who had put him down? The woman or the hooded figure in gray?

"How? Who? . . . . What?" he said.

The figure in gray pulled back its hood.

Gabriel steeled himself.

They slowly raised their hands to their head and gently removed the mask. From ground level, the face was hard to discern.

"Hello, Mike," it said.

Only one person would call him Mike, the name he used when hanging around the bars gathering intelligence. "Katie?"

CHAPTER FIVE

THE CRUTCHES BENEATH Gabriel's arms dug into his armpits. They were old, wooden, and little uneven. Katie had told him to use them and not ask any questions. Her and the woman walked on either side of Gabriel and led him in the dim lighting to the closed door of his room.

"Why didn't you tell me it was you?" Gabriel asked.

"It wasn't my time, Mike . . . . Gabriel."

It sounded weird, her saying his real name, but at this point, what was there to do?

"Katie, if Redsaw is controlling you or manipulating you somehow . . . I mean, you were there. You didn't interfere. You watched as . . . as . . ."

"I'm sorry, Gabriel."

As if. I know you well enough that you play it smart so even if Redsaw is controlling you, you're probably biding your time for an escape. "Sorry's not good enough."

Katie remained silent, arms at her sides, mask held in one hand. Her blonde hair was tied back in what looked like an uncomfortably-tight bun, probably solely for the sake of the mask.

They were at the door to the room, Gabriel standing in the dim light. He reached out and touched the door. Its density suggested the wooden door was thick and old, which meant the wood could very well have been terribly aged thus making it like cement.

"So what's the next step? You guys take a cripple to another torture chamber now that he's strong enough so you could break him down again?" he asked.

"Something like that," the woman said.

Gabriel looked her way then shot Katie a glare to be sure she knew he wasn't impressed. But, right now, on crutches and without his powers, he had no choice but to obey.

"All I'm going to say, Katie, is I would have expected better from you," he said.

She didn't reply. She looked to the woman, who opened the door.

The hallway beyond was the opposite of the room they were in: Smooth, eggshell-painted walls, elegant tiled flooring. Bright lights overhead lit everything in an ivory glow that was soothing to the eyes.

Gabriel furrowed his brow. Looked back at the room then back at the hallway. "What the heck?"

The three stepped out into the hallway and Gabriel peered in both directions. They seemed to be in the middle of a long hallway. One end was a good fifty to seventy feet away, but it was hard to tell as his eyes adjusted to the light. The hall seemed to stop at a wall that had its own hallway running perpendicular to the one they were in. To his left and right, the hall held more doorways, some opposite each other, each painted the dark blue of his Axiom-man uniform.

This didn't make sense. How could Redsaw afford this? Who did he take this place away from? Did he customize the doors just to get under his skin? Gabriel's head went a little fuzzy from the questions. He adjusted his position on the crutches so he was more comfortable.

"Welcome home, Gabriel," the woman said.

———

They led Gabriel down the hallway to the end and turned right. He asked to pause for a moment to gather up some strength but was denied.

At the end of the second hallway, they went right again. Soon they reached a set of double doors, these painted the same blue with a chrome panel about a foot tall and half a foot wide on each door where the handles should be. He expected they were like swinging hospital doors that opened in either direction. The woman urged him close to the doors with a little-but-sharp tug on his shoulder.

She pointed to the chrome panel. "Touch."

He glanced at the woman then at Katie. This was it. This was the trap. This was Redsaw showing off and making him feel truly isolated and helpless. Slowly, he put his palm forward and placed it on the panel.

The doors opened.

"Oooh-kay," he said. When he took his eyes off his hands, there was another set of double doors about ten feet ahead. These were silver and appeared very secure.

The trio approached the doors with another set of chrome panels. Gabriel looked to the woman. She nodded. He put his palm to the panel and the half-a-foot-thick doors opened inward into a vast room that looked like a gym but with some apparatuses he didn't recognize. Was this some sort of sick joke? Was Redsaw going to have these two torture him with exercise equipment? Outside of the creativity, this was nuts.

"You're going to have to drag me in there. I'm not moving," he said.

Katie put a gentle hand on his shoulder. "Gabriel, I want you to look at her."

"Why?"

"Please trust me."

He looked down at his feet and the bottoms of the crutches on either side. He nodded and raised his face to the woman. Though he didn't want to admit it, her beauty was captivating. Her pitch-black hair ran long and straight down her back. Her deep green eyes were without a flaw in their color. Her face was smooth in feature but her jaw was firm. And her body—this was clearly a woman who kept in shape and had the curves, solidity, and musculature to back it up. Her clothes were simple with what appeared to be a common woman's body suit with a black torso and gray arms and legs. Thigh-high, black boots wrapped her legs. He noticed the boots didn't have any heels. Was this a costume? Was she a . . . a metahuman? Were her and Katie some sort of costumed combatants? Did Redsaw demand they wear outfits outside normal civilian clothing so they'd stand out and those looking on would know they were separate? Even possibly conveying a message by their attire they worked for him?

"I am Aiyesha Elnaa," she said. "You will refer to me as Mistress."

He looked to Katie. "Does she know how that sounds?"

"The mistress does, and the mistress doesn't care. You will address her as requested."

"What's wrong with you?" he said.

Katie gazed at the woman. Gabriel finally did the same.

"We are not who you think we are, Gabriel," she said.

Gabriel wanted to say he knew exactly who Katie was and that the question was semi-rhetorical, but he kept his mouth shut.

"We are your allies, Gabriel," Aiyesha said.

"By keeping me in a coffin? By starving me and barely allowing me to survive? By humiliating me against some stupid wooden wall, a *red* wall, just so, what, you can bring me here and do . . . do . . ." There were so many directions to take the question.

"Welcome to the Central, Gabriel," Aiyesha said. "Your home."

"My—"

"This place is for you, Gabriel," Katie said. "Here, you will learn who you truly are. Here, is where you'll begin to make your stand."

"My . . . stand?"

"Against Redsaw, against the other metas, against the evil of the world," Aiyesha said.

"I thought I was already doing that?"

"To defeat. We—I will teach you to conquer so they will not be a threat again."

Gabriel said, "I'm not going to kill them." Then quietly added, "Not like it was a real option the first time, anyway."

"Then you have already learned your first lesson."

"Lesson?"

"Come with me."

CHAPTER SIX

THREE WEEKS LATER.

Six hundred and seventy-four. Six hundred and seventy-five. Each slam of Gabriel's fist into the Wing Chun dummy sent a shockwave of hot pain through his knuckles and hand. And this was only his right hand. His left was occupied executing a block to the dummy's wooden arm while his right plowed into where a person's face would be.

Aiyesha.

She was merciless. Katie nursed him back to health, so he was well enough to begin training. Gabriel knew he needed more time to heal but extra time was forbidden. Aiyesha wanted to start working the moment he was able. And it had been in the middle of the night while he was asleep that she came, cut off his air supply with a grip to his throat, then told him to get up when he was choked awake. The lights were out and Gabriel was told to sense her presence in front of him and follow her in the dark. He tried but kept losing her only to hear annoyance in her voice when he did.

"If you would turn on the lights, Mistress, I could—" She clutched his throat before he could finish speaking. He swung his fist but just before he connected, she slipped her head away and he swept through nothing but air. Quickly, she pulled his arm straight, twisted, and had him bent at the waist with severe pressure against his shoulder joint. Tears immediately came to his eyes.

"I said to follow me. I do not know how I can be any clearer," she said.

His shoulder begged to be relieved of the agony. "But . . . but the lights."

"If you rely only on your eyes, you will miss more than you are now willing to accept. You will listen to me and do as I say." She increased the pressure against his shoulder and Gabriel howled. "Understood?"

"Yes . . . Mistress. I'm . . . I'm sorry."

"Good."

She released him but it took nearly an hour for the pain inflicted to ease up. She must have found a nerve center while simultaneously putting pressure on the joint.

They entered the facility with the equipment. The lights went on.

"You will spend your time here. Each day, every day until I say otherwise. Once your day is complete, you will return to your quarters to rest. In the morning, you will come here. If you do not come here, I will come and retrieve you and what you just experienced will be but a light touch in comparison."

This wasn't right. This was ridiculous. He was Axiom-man. He had conquered more than a mere mortal who knew some kind of martial arts. He. Was. Powerful.

"You are arrogant," she said, as if reading his mind. "You have thought yourself special because of what you could do. You relied on your gifts daily to get through from dawn to sunset. This is unacceptable."

"Yeah? Then what about the *surges* and increase in power? The messenger said I was rewarded with more ability because I used my powers properly."

"If you used your powers properly, Redsaw would have been defeated. You were given excess from the messenger to lead you in that direction. Instead, below the surface, you grew in pride and that pride cost you your love, your city, and, worst of all, yourself."

"I have no idea what you're talking about, and how do you know the messenger?"

"See? That is the problem, Gabriel Garrison. You do not know." Her green eyes shot him a fiery stare.

"How could you say that? I basically died trying to stop him. I took beatings upon beatings to save my city and those I love. I fought people who would destroy the average man and prevailed. I kept those other metas at bay while my city burned. You have no right to—"

Gabriel was on the floor, looking up at her through hazy vision, completely unsure how he wound up on his back. The rear of his skull stung, no doubt from the impact.

"You will not disrespect me again."

"Take her advice, Gabriel," Katie said, still in uniform, unmasked, standing just behind the top of his head. "Mistress, am I permitted to speak freely?"

Permitted? What did she do to Katie? Brainwash her?

"You are permitted," Aiyesha said.

Katie crouched down and leaned close to Gabriel's face. "Gabriel," she said softly.

He groaned. "What?"

"Do you trust me?"

"I don't know."

"Have I ever given you any reason not to?"

"You're interacting with her like you're some kind of drone. What did she do to you?"

Katie waited a moment before speaking. "She changed me. Made the Night Fowler."

"Night Fowler?"

"What you see before you. *You*, Gabriel, created me initially. Showed me what could be possible to help others. The Mistress took what you started and completed it."

"I will not be programmed."

"You won't be. You will be made better, but first you have to yield. You have to lay the cape aside. Take the mask off. Remove the uniform."

"If you've been paying attention, Katie, I'm not wearing any of that."

"Don't be hopeless. I was obviously not referring to your clothing. Think."

He knew what she meant but it was hard to swallow. To make it worse, he knew she was right. Axiom-man had gotten in the way of himself. He didn't even know who he was anymore between identities and Valerie, and the public, and flying to help people, and so much more. Though his head was mostly ablur from the impact, Katie's words were clear.

He had to start over.

"Empty your cup, Gabriel. Pour it out. Let go," Katie said.

"I don't know how."

"You do. It's not instant, but if you work at humbling yourself and admitting you need help and open yourself to learning, you will become your Axiom."

Nine hundred and ninety-eight. Smack. *Nine hundred and ninety-nine.* Smack. *One thousand.* Gabriel looked at his bloody knuckles. He carefully and slowly opened his fingers, stretching out a hand that had been a fist for most of the day. His left forearm ached from blocking against the wooden dummy, and he had yet to change hands even after seven hours of striking the wood. He was not to leave until he executed one thousand repetitions of a basic combination against the dummy.

On both sides.

He closed his eyes, refocused and adjusted his stance.

He shot out his left hand while simultaneously blocking with his right. His right-hand knuckles spat droplets of blood into the air until the flow stopped and things coagulated. *One.* Smack. *Two.* Smack.

Three.

It was going to be an even longer day.

———

Aiyesha was there just as he was finishing. When he completed his task, he turned to her, bowed slightly at the waist, and said, "Mistress."

"Gabriel." She stepped up to the dummy and inspected it. He didn't know what she was looking for. The wood remained solid, the deep brick red of his blood smeared on its surface. She pointed to it. "Your form was incorrect."

"How can you tell?"

"I can see your strikes, see your blood." She turned to him, eyes stern. "You were shown last week how to do it properly and yet you still err."

Err? "I did what I knew how to do. I did as you asked, Mistress."

She folded her hands behind her back, stepped away from the dummy, then walked past him. "Good," she said. "Now do it right."

She left the room.

Gabriel looked at his swelling hands, his knuckles nothing but peeled open and dark red.

He closed his eyes and shoved away the aching fatigue.

Gabriel set his feet, arms and hands. *One.* Smack. *Two.* Smack.

Three.

————

Two days later.

Gabriel was awakened by a bucket of ice water. His ears went instantly numb and the shock from the sudden cold slamming into a warm bed made his head momentarily swim and all he could do was shiver. He sat up, took a second, then sat at the edge of the bed. It wasn't fancy. A thin mattress with an equally-thin pillow and a rough wool blanket. "Thanks," he muttered.

Aiyesha stood there, an old tin bucket swinging by the handle in her grip. She tossed a gray sweat suit at him. "Get dressed. Follow me."

Gabriel knew by now any hesitation would land him in trouble, so he quickly tore off his sopping wet and cold clothes and put on the sweat suit. She eyed him the whole time and he couldn't help but wonder if her doing so was either common where she came from or if she was trying to humiliate him again.

He followed her down the hall as if heading to the training area. Instead, they stopped at a plain door with a normal knob, no indication on the door as to what was behind it. She turned the knob and hit a light switch to illuminate the room. Buzzing neon lights shone over the cement-walled room with the worn-out brown carpet. Some of the lights flickered; one was burnt out. The room ran approximately twenty or so feet square and all it contained was rustic, old-school iron weights and bars.

"You will grow strong here," she said. "This is where we'll start, but this is not where we will end."

Gabriel looked around the room. It was a dive. He could hardly read the poundage on some of the metal plates. The only decoration was a standard eight-and-a-half-by-eleven piece of dirty white paper with faded black lettering that read:

Pick it up
Put it down
Repeat

"I don't understand," he said. "There's a perfectly good modern gym in the next room. Why here in this dump?"

"If you do not know by now, it makes me wonder if the messenger chose the right person. I will show you proper technique for the base exercises I want you to do. You will do them as I show you to avoid injury and to increase progress. You will start with weight lighter than you can handle to ensure your form is correct. After that, and with my approval, you will increase the weight, and this room will become a part of your life for the next term."

"Term?"

"This is part of the Acceleration."

"Acceleration? Like, ultra speed or something?"

She stared at him for a long while. It was as if she didn't understand the question, but Gabriel understood it to mean be quiet, do what you're told, and stop questioning the method.

"To use a metaphor you will understand," she said, Gabriel suddenly feeling small, "we are laying out pieces to a puzzle in order to build a picture."

That's what puzzles are, he thought. Why did she have to talk down to him?

"Except," she continued, "the final picture is being hidden from you for now. Should you be aware of it at this moment, it would interfere with our work."

"How?"

"Silence." The firmness in her voice was enough to send a jolt through him. She didn't even have to shout. "A day will come when you will see the pieces in clarity and understanding and wisdom will come upon you. But until that day, until it is revealed, you will continue to do as I say, when I say it, and how I say to do it. The questions will cease effective immediately. The only questions permitted will be those relating to the work we are doing. Anything further or not yet ready to be revealed will not be discussed." She turned her deep green eyes toward him and bore her stare into him. "Understood? Do not say yes if it is not true."

The Acceleration. What did she mean by that? It was too late now to fight or resist. Not that he would stand a chance anyway. Obviously, she was working on him for a reason and citing the messenger, even though it made him feel bad, only cemented that fact. There was no choice but to do as he was told.

It was time to let go.

It was time to trust.

It was time to do what needed to be done.

"Yes, Mistress," he said. "I understand."

Chapter Seven

Gabriel was careful lowering the barbell from a bicep curl.

"Be mindful of the negative," his Mistress had said. Lowering the barbell with control and slowness focused a different effort on the muscle so he gained strength both on the lift itself and on the lowering of it.

His gray sweatsuit stuck to his sweat-coated body like a second skin. But he didn't care.

"Start doing this long enough and you will feel better," his Mistress had said. She explained the chemistry changes in the body from the exercise. Some stuff Gabriel knew, other aspects he didn't. But she had been right. He *was* feeling better. Much better. The only part of training he didn't like was the uncomfortable warmth as his body heated up during exercise until his skin finally burst forth soothing drops of sweat to cool him down. Once he was soaked, his temperature was completely comfortable, but he always had a thing against being *that* uncomfortably warm. It happened when the seasons changed and you were torn between dressing up or dressing down because Winnipeg weather seemed to change every hour on the hour.

Gabriel exhaled upon exertion and brought the bar up, contracting the muscles. He was instructed to give the muscle a squeeze upon apex of the movement then, without breaking tension, begin the process of working on the negative.

"You will do them strict. You will do them right," she had said.

"Yes, Mistress." That was his reply. That was always his reply. Stating otherwise seemed like backtalking to a parent and was always met with a stare that chilled him. Whoever she was, there was something in those green eyes that said not to test her or push her on any level. He just hoped he was keeping on his side of the fence while he did as instructed.

For the first while, his main focus was on getting the motion and form right for each exercise. He was to start light, even if he could lift more, and then work his way up to more weight once she approved of his form. From there, he did as told, sometimes able to squeeze out an extra repetition for Valerie.

I miss you, he thought, lowering the bar. *Every day. Every moment.* Her beautiful face appeared in his thoughts, her deep brown eyes and gorgeous brown hair that flowed down her head and onto her shoulders with such grace.

Then she was gone and his Mistress's voice filled his head: "Focus."

Valerie . . . "Yes, Mistress."

––––––––––

It was morning. Early. Gabriel wasn't allowed to have a clock so he didn't know exactly what time it was, but his internal clock told him it was early and he needed to go to the gym.

He entered the cement-walled room and turned on the light. He still wasn't completely sure why this gym was being used instead of the state-of-the-art facility in the other room. He could only suppose his Mistress wanted to toughen him up by setting him in such a grungy environment.

I've been in worse, he thought, then checked himself. It was pride his mistress was trying to strip from him. Unhealthy self-reliance, a pattern he had slipped into without realizing he had been on the descent.

Gabriel proceeded to the dumbbell rack and grabbed pair of five-pounders. These were to warm up the shoulders. Just as he was about to start slow shoulder circles, Aiyesha entered the room.

"Stop," she said softly but firmly.

He set the dumbbells down on the floor then stood straight. "Morning, Mistress."

"It's 'Good morning,' Gabriel. Speak in full sentences."

"I'm sorry, Mistress."

She raised her hand and signaled him over with a wave of her finger. "Come." She made her way to the squat rack. The barbell wasn't in its usual place but was instead on the floor. On each side were six forty-five-pound black plates. "Did you notice this upon entry?"

He looked at the barbell. "No, Mistress. Only now when you pointed it out."

"Learn to be more observant of your surroundings."

He nodded.

She looked at the bar. "Can you lift this?"

Gabriel did the math. Five hundred and forty pounds. Yes, he could lift it.

If he had his powers.

He slowly shook his head. "No."

"Why not?"

"I'm not strong enough nor big enough. I haven't trained long enough, and to lift something this heavy would take years for someone like me to work up to."

"I'm glad you recognize that. You live in an instant-gratification society, Gabriel. It's the hard truth of your current place in time."

Current place in time?

"The martial way is not instant. It is a lifetime practice, and even then, can never be mastered. Perhaps" —she seemed to smile at her own words— "if one were immortal it would be possible, but humans are finite, therefore mastery is beyond your grasp. However, highly-tuned skill can be obtained." She pointed to the barbell. "Pick it up."

Gabriel looked to the side then back at her.

"Now," she said.

"Yes, Mistress." He went to the middle of the bar, centered his feet and sturdied himself, then grabbed the bar evenly with both hands. He glanced up at her.

"Pick it up," she said.

Does she know something I don't? Do I have my powers back? Oh man, this could be it. This could be— He tried to lift the bar and the thing did not budge. He also felt some strain run through his back. He carefully stood to avoid injuring himself. "I'm sorry, but I cannot lift it."

"Try again. This time attempt to use your whole body. I've already shown you how to do what you term a 'deadlift.' Do it to that bar."

He knew better than to question her a second time so again he got himself ready, made sure his hand positioning was correct, the right grip, the right stance, mind focused on lifting the bar.

He pulled against it, trying to bring it upward. It did not move and his body was locked in a static tension of full-body muscle use.

"Stop," she said. He started to ease up on the bar. "No, maintain your position and lift." Gabriel got right back to attempting to lift it. All that ran through him were burning muscles that didn't have the strength. "Keep trying," she said, "and pay attention. What you are feeling now running through your body would be considered a full-body effort to lift a heavy object. Notice how you are using your legs, your arms, your glutes—how your whole body is involved with the lift."

Muscles burning from the pull, Gabriel nodded, sweat starting to bead across his forehead.

"Don't stop."

Fire through his muscles.

"Pay attention to your body. Feel its full force trying to lift the barbell."

He felt it and then some, but he explored as instructed. Felt the exertion in his legs, the pull in his arms, how his whole body seemed trapped in the effort to hoist the heavy object.

"Let go," she said.

He eased up slowly, giving the muscles a chance to loosen before relaxing entirely. When he stood, his head swooned and she went out of focus for a moment before returning to clarity.

"Whole body," she said. "We will now use this as you learn to power the skills I will teach you so that when executed, not mere strength is used as you are so used to, but power. Power is the body. Strength is the muscles. There is a difference."

At first, he didn't catch on but then realized she was talking about the body working in unison with itself, one area not solely relying on the other to accomplish something.

"Today you start a new term," she said. "Today, we will begin to use what you just attempted to your advantage."

"Advantage for what?"
"Power."

———

In the main facility, there was a blue mat in the center of the room approximately twenty-feet square. Aiyesha had Gabriel positioned in the middle of it.

"You have the overview on a few things," she said. "Now we learn the details." She took his hand in hers, turned it palm-up, then said, "Make a fist."

He did.

"No, make a fist."

"I just—"

She unfolded his hand and, step-by-step, showed him how to properly curl his fingers inward, how to maintain a straight wrist and how to make his knuckles square. This fist was not what he was used to, yet it felt more natural, more aligned. Not that his regular fist was inefficient. He had delivered many blows with it over the years, but this fist seemed more secure, more solid. It only reinforced the idea he'd been relying on his ultra strength too much to do the job.

"Begin. Sitting stand punch. Hyke!"

Gabriel drew his leg out, split his weight fifty-fifty and threw out a punch.

"The overview," she said. "Your technique is horrible."

He didn't think it was too bad but who was he to argue with her? "So what of all the punching against the wooden dummy? Why do that if it was incorrect?"

"No, for that I showed you the correct way. You were the one who made it incorrect, but what you did accomplish was building the not-often-used muscles needed for proper execution. Today, all day, you will conduct sitting stance punches. I will watch you. I will correct you. You will perform the strike until you get it right, and then you will do it right until your muscles decide to make your form sloppy. Then you will stop. Understood?"

"Yes, Mistress."

"Let's begin."

She led him to the gym's mirror and told him to take his stance. Gabriel obeyed.

"Half speed, half power. Show me execution," she said.

Gabriel punched as he had been originally shown, even in this posture focusing on putting power behind his punch. He threw out his arm. Before he could switch to punch with the other, she stopped him with a raise of her hand. Firmly yet gently, she made a small adjustment to ensure his wrist was straight and slightly adjusted his aim to what would be an opponent's middle. "Proceed," she said.

Gabriel put out his other arm, this time doing his best to make sure the strike followed what she just showed him with the small adjustments.

"Better," she said. "Keep going. I will tell you when to pick up speed. Focus on your technique in this basic strike and, if you get that right, it will aid in all other strikes to come."

He nodded.

"Again."

He punched.

"Again."

He punched.

"Again."

He punched.

"Again."

———

The term lasted thirty days, each day focusing on a single technique. One movement per side of his body. For the entire month, he did not learn a single kick. Only strikes and blocks. He would start slow and careful after being shown, accept Aiyesha's correction then enact it on the next effort. He performed each simple strike or block until, as she had said, his muscles fatigued and his form began to slip. It was only then he was allowed to stop, eat, drink, stretch and give each arm a rest. Once his strength was gathered, the day would continue with the same single technique, over and over. He did not keep count of how many times he did it per day, but he was sure each technique must have been practiced at least two to three thousand times per day. By the time each day was over, he couldn't even stomach the thought of that particular move. Too much. But this was part of the acceleration process, he knew. She was drilling muscle memory into him to an extreme extent, having him do the technique right ad nauseum. Aiyesha was with him throughout it all, watching, correcting, adjusting, commending. How she was not bored supervising him all day, he didn't know.

It seemed combat was her life and that she knew nothing else. He wondered about Katie and where she had gone. When he had asked Aiyesha about her roughly two weeks back, all his Mistress said was, "None of your concern." That was it. An ice-cold answer.

Today was day thirty-one of the term, and it was early and they were in the gym.

"Today, we review," Aiyesha said.

Gabriel nodded.

"I will ask. You will do."

He nodded again.

"Sitting stance punch."

Immediately Gabriel did a small arc with his right leg, bringing it out into position and as he sat down in the stance, threw out his right fist.

"Good," she said. "Other side."

He did.

"Good. Again."

He obeyed.

"Again."

He did so.

"Right foot back, left forearm front guarding block."

He executed the guard.

"Switch."

He changed sides.

"Switch."

He did it again.

"Switch."

And again.

"Right arm, right foot forward, low guarding block."

He switched his feet, stepped forward and in a smooth arc executed the technique. She made a small adjustment by moving his forearm a mere few millimeters outward.

"Other side. Switch."

He did and executed it with his left.

"Switch."

He did.

"Turn, one-hundred-eighty degrees and execute."

He carefully minded his feet, rotated to face the other side of the room and put out the block.

"Forward."

He did, blocking again.

"Inward-outward forearm front guarding block."

He did. And for each technique, she had him do it several times. Sometimes he thought she would move to another technique on the list, but sometimes she doubled back, asking him to do something he had already performed.

"Left hand high punch."

He did.

"Left hand low punch followed by right high back fist."

He did.

"Left hook, left back fist."

He did.

"Right hook, right back fist."

He did.

"Sitting stance straight punch."

He did.

"Right walking stance high block."

He did.

And did.

And did.

———

The term was over and Gabriel was allowed one day to rest, but it was not a day of leisure. He had to follow his diet and was instructed to nap for precisely one and a half hours. He didn't know how she could time that factoring in the normal time it took to fall asleep, but he did as he was told. When he awoke, it turned out she timed him once he went under and woke him when the time was up.

He was to stretch and to consciously relax his upper extremities as much as able.

When it was time for bed, despite the rest, it felt like he had put in a full day. Falling asleep was not hard at all.

———

The next morning after a protein-infused smoothie breakfast, Gabriel was taken to the main facility. When the blue doors opened, Aiyesha pointed to the black, metal staircase to the far left he hadn't noticed the first time he saw the room.

The stairs led up to a second level, which was a running track that circled the facility.

Once at the top and on the track, Aiyesha pointed to the right. "That direction. Walk. When I say, switch to a light jog. When I say again, you jog fully. When I say run, you run as fast as you can for as long as you can. Understood?"

"Yes, Mistress."

"Good," she said. "Now walk."

Gabriel began his way around the track. The floor was flat with a thin layer of carpeting. He glanced back at Aiyesha; her eyes were on him on the whole time. An unsettling twist entered his stomach. Her eyes, though beautiful, were worth their weight in iron. He thought of Valerie's eyes, that look of helplessness on her face as the world went inferno around her.

"Switch!"

He picked up his pace. His city—he hadn't been there for so long. Redsaw could be doing anything. The world—as far as he knew, the entire planet—beyond these walls could be dead.

And he would have failed twice over. He didn't know how to bring it up with Aiyesha.

"Switch!"

Gabriel went into a full jog and rounded the curved corner of the track. Was Katie out there, helping out somehow? How did she get that outfit? What happened to her after she faked her death? Where did she go? Who did she see? How did she connect with Aiyesha?

Katie was always an endless list of questions and she proved to be the same now.

Gabriel rounded the corner where Aiyesha stood.

"Now run," she said.

The world needed him. Even a dead world because even then, even if Redsaw was all who was left, he needed to be removed from the planet. If all this training needed to be about one thing, that would be it.

He fixed his eyes forward.

Gabriel ran.

CHAPTER EIGHT

TERM TWO LASTED a month as well.

The worst month.

One kick per day. One hour practicing with one leg, one hour practicing the same technique with the other, then switching back to the other leg to repeat. It was also during Term Two his training became his entire day. He'd wake, eat a nutritious breakfast or have a smoothie, was allowed ten minutes for it to settle, then hit the track for an hour. After, a stretching session with Aiyesha and then onto the kicking technique for the day. Once the day was done, he'd stumble on rubbery legs to the cement gym to work that day's body part. Then a walk around the track, then slow down time and sleep.

That first kicking lesson made him feel like a child with the way she treated him, but he also understood that in this arena, he *was* a child and his mistress ran the show and how dare he even attempt to question her methods.

"Very basic," she said. "This is called a front kick." Her leg left the floor in a blur, did something while raised, then was back down before Gabriel could grasp exactly what she had done.

"I—"

"Look and focus." She brought her leg up, knee bent. "Your knee is like a sight on a bow."

"Bow?"

"Bow and arrow."

"Like a gun?"

She frowned. "I will not refer to those weapons. They are a coward's choice. They are also the reason your world is in constant peril. People with power, they wield a coward's weapon to control because they themselves do not possess the skill to maintain their particular brand of order. No. What we do here is more important than that, and you are better than that. If you let yourself be." She added that last statement with a slight smile in her voice. It was out of character but Gabriel didn't care. He'd take any encouragement he could right now. "As I was saying," she said, "where your knee is pointed is where your kick will land. This applies to nearly all leg techniques. If you understand this and use your knee for accuracy, you will excel through what we need to cover and, frankly, you need to pick up your pace."

Pick up my pace? My days are laid out by you. I don't understand what you mean by—no, he got it. The message was loud and clear. He needed to search deep within and pull out his best effort, his best focus, his best ability to absorb something new. "Yes, Mistress."

"Your knee joint only bends one way thus why it is important for aim." She shot the lower part of her leg out slow enough for him to see. She held her foot aloft. Her toes were bent back, and even through the boots she wore, it was clear she was using the ball of the foot to complete the execution. "I do not need to explain, do I?"

"I do not know how to answer that. I want to learn what you have to teach." He paused. "May I speak freely?"

She nodded.

"You use your knee to line up your shot and then when you extend your leg, you are placing the ball of your foot where you intend it to land."

"That is correct, Gabriel. Good." She used her eyes to direct his back to her leg. "To withdraw, bending your knee back in for this kick is effective when given with a snap." She shot her leg back out and then retracted it quickly, her leg still raised and bent at the knee. "And then place." She straightened her leg as she brought it behind her into a graceful fighting stance.

"Your turn."

Gabriel set himself in the guard. "Slow?"

"Slow."

He brought up his knee, watching its end, then extended his leg, ensuring the ball of his foot was used as the striking tool. He drew his leg back in then lowered it slightly behind him and set himself back in guard.

"Not a bad first effort. Let's sharpen your technique and then you will practice this technique until you are told otherwise. Do you understand?"

"Yes, Mistress, I understand."

"Let's proceed."

———

Gabriel learned on Day Seventeen that a kick can be used with a straight leg and did not always need to be executed through a bend in the knee. He was taught a high kick, which was a straight raising of the leg, the aim being to land the ball of his foot under someone's chin, similar to an uppercut, but to continue following through with the leg thus sending the opponent's head back, leaving them vulnerable for other technique execution. He was also cautioned this particular kick, as simple as it was, needed to have the right timing and the right distance otherwise another technique would need to be chosen.

The straight kick he particularly liked was its opposite, what she dubbed an "axe kick." It was the same thing—a quick rise of the leg—but the force was executed on the way down, the heel being the main tool.

"If you time the axe kick correctly and are at proper distance, and, once learned correctly, you can use it break a collarbone or shoulder. Even end a life if you land it on the appropriate nerve center by the neck. You will cause the muscles to cramp and tighten thus putting pressure on what you know as the windpipe. That will be for an extraordinary scenario and takes time to learn how to do it with enough power for the optimal outcome. But even not at full power, it can cause the same end: taking away someone's breath."

That's harsh, he thought, but he also understood he was being taught a technique that can be used with a spectrum of power, everything from a small tap to a violent and deadly blow. How much power to use would take learning and, over time and experience, discernment.

Gabriel executed axe kick number four hundred-three onto the potato sack filled with rice on the floor. His left leg was burning from the repetition, but if it was focus and faster learning she wanted, that was what Aiyesha was going to get.

There was no time to play games.

There was no time to take it slow.

There was only time to work.

Gabriel brought up his leg then swiftly brought it down. The skin on his heel was raw from striking the rough burlap potato sack. No matter. It was time for calluses anyway.

It was time to prove to her that his being Axiom-man was not a mistake.

It was time to prove—some way, somehow—he was not a failure.

Gabriel kicked again.

And again.

TRANSFORMATIONS

———

Term Three.

It was basic to start. Aiyesha would show him three-strike combinations utilizing his hands and feet. Jab, punch, front kick. Right hook, right back fist, use the clinch and plow your knee into your opponent's gut. Straight punch, turning kick one leg, turning kick the other.

And so it went. Each day the same assigned three-strike combination over and over until his form ran sloppy. He did notice, however, that as time went on, he was able to hold correct form longer and longer. The day he lasted an hour longer than usual was the day he aimed for two extra hours on the next. That was a mistake. But he did make it to the hour-and-a-half mark. After that, it was as if everything he had learned left him and he had nothing to offer but sloppy, noodle-like strikes that a child could fend off.

Aiyesha did not berate him for it. Instead, she said, "This is growth. This is the point of martial art. This is you rising." It appeared as if she was going to say something further but stopped herself. No matter. Perhaps she didn't want to build him up too far.

Then she continued. "Humbleness and humility are among the first tenets of the creed I follow. You must be meek and gentle, for this will bring peace. The combat, that is also for peace, but gentleness and kindness are your most powerful weapons. It is better to not strike than to strike. It is better to grant life than to kill. It is more important to remain humble in heart than to bring yourself high because of your own power."

She sounds almost biblical, Gabriel thought as he worked on rushing in with an elbow on one side to the chin, then the same with the other, then a knife-hand strike to the throat.

If he was certain of anything, it was Aiyesha *was* changing him, *was* making him more, but, as per her tutelage, he stuffed that knowledge away and did not dwell on it so as to remain focused on task and humble in heart.

Gabriel took to the heavy bag with as much aggression yet finesse as he could.

"Technique always wins over strength," Aiyesha had told him.

He kept that in mind as he executed his punches and kicks. At first, striking the bag was difficult, which surprised him since he was used to hitting bad guys with ease. But that was with his powers. Now, it was just him: one human against two hundred pounds of swinging weight. He had thought his punches—especially with the strength training—would make more of a dent in the bag, but hitting the sand, packed good and tight beneath the canvas and almost solid but with enough give to absorb the blow, was no different than flesh on bone.

"This bag will develop muscles you do not know you have," she had said. And she had been right. Each day, slugging the bag left him sore in new places. Tiny little muscle groups around his major muscle groups burned and ached. After a week, the discomfort finally went away and he wasn't as sore the day after.

Punch. Punch. Knife hand strike. Elbow. Knee. Clinch. Knee again, other side. Push off with a push kick then send two front kicks into the belly followed by a turning kick to the head.

Each bag session had its own program: specific strikes in specific combinations. The concept was teach him to put techniques together then, once he finished her combinations, to make up combinations of his own in the interest of improving improvisation. He had to admit these multiple striking patterns were new to execute and to endure. With his powers, even against a metahuman opponent, the fights did not last as long as his sessions with the bag. These sessions were hours. His other fights much less than that, even the difficult ones.

This was about endurance.

This was about patience.

This was about putting thought into each technique.

When Aiyesha watched him improvise, she didn't say anything though Gabriel expected correction at any moment. Even his first efforts in front of her were clumsy solely because he didn't like the idea of being watched, though he should have been used to it. Simply, he was afraid to upset her, get corrected yet again, and be told he did everything wrong. Instead, she merely watched. Did not correct form. Did not correct execution. Did not correct anything.

Probably assessing, he thought. *Then you'll be in for it.* He shoved the idea away and pretended she wasn't there. No, he couldn't do that. He had to maintain awareness of his surroundings and being aware of those present was part of that. So he acknowledged her presence then kept her in his peripheral as he worked the bag, as if she was a shadow and nothing more.

If anything was consistently sore, it was his hands despite wearing leather bag gloves. The constant pummeling of the canvas made his knuckles ache and sometimes made it difficult for him to open his fists as his fingers would cramp. But he learned to relax, to tighten up at the last possible microsecond upon execution of the blow then relax again on the speedy retraction.

"Always remain fluid," she said off to the side.

"Yes, Mistress." He attacked the bag again, sending a crescent kick along its side followed by a reverse crescent kick with the other leg. When his foot struck the canvas, the bag gave in a little and Gabriel understood right then the power of momentum and speed.

This was physics. And geometry.

Too bad I flunked those, he thought. But it didn't matter. Aiyesha was teaching him the concepts anew and he was learning.

Quickly.

———

A month later and Gabriel was taken to the mat in the main facility.

"You have been taught your techniques through traditional methods. While you would have noticed the stances and execution in traditional forms are not how you would move and execute in a combat scenario" —she raised a finger, cementing the point— "traditional forms are where you get your power from. They are designed the way they are for that reason. It teaches you draw within yourself—all that you are—and channel it through the limb that is executing the technique. Now, after learning combinations on the heavy bag and wooden dummy, you will step back and practice through traditional form."

"Mistress?"

"Yes?"

"Why did we not start combinations through traditional form first?"

"Because I did not want to hinder your progress. Understand, Gabriel, that while these forms are important, nothing can compare to human instinct and spirit, human determination and fluidity. I wanted you to feel yourself as you worked your techniques. I wanted you to learn what a strike felt like and for you to practice improvisation without restriction. Martial art is as much study and skill as it is imagination and improvisation. With those elements combined—*when* they are combined—you will become a very dangerous person."

The way she nuanced those last two words sent a shockwave of encouragement and motivation through Gabriel's system. "And we are studying to conquer Redsaw, are we not?"

She bowed her head as if disappointed. "We are studying for you to conquer yourself. You cannot hope to overcome another if you cannot overcome your own shortcomings. In this case, your failure to apprehend him and what it did to you . . . and to others."

His heart stung and a flash of anger bubbled within. She had no right to talk to him like that. But she *was* right. Throughout his training, throughout observing and notating his thoughts, his movements, his feelings—the more he was brought low, the more he understood he could have been a better Axiom-man. That, maybe, he had been the wrong recipient of those powers several years ago. Yet that couldn't be true either. The messenger had told him he was the only option to receive those abilities, the last in a line of heritage capable of receiving and using those abilities. It was either him or no one. The issue now was . . . was he still Axiom-man? He was told he wasn't. Told he had failed. Told he had someone to answer to.

But it wasn't Redsaw.

It was someone worse.

CHAPTER NINE

THE MONTH OF traditional forms felt like six. Each movement was scrutinized to the most minor detail, even so much as adjusting his arm a mere millimeter more to the right or left. Aiyesha stayed on him day after day, hour after hour, minute after minute, blasted second by blasted second. He was not allowed to learn a new pattern of techniques until he locked down the one currently being taught.

Each technique was executed from proper posture, proper stance, proper baseline technique. As he stepped forward in a walking stance with a punch then executed a low block with the other hand, Aiyesha said, "Remember your rhythm. It is like . . . it is like your culture and your dancing. Use a beat as you strike. One and two, and one and two, and one and—do you understand?"

"Yes, Mistress."

Gabriel counted off his next move as if about to join a waltz but striking to a beat didn't come as awkwardly as he first thought. If anything, it made performing the forms much easier.

"You know you will have stepped correctly when you finish at the same point you started," she said. "Each form functions inside its own geometric shape for this purpose. Remember your start. Mind your footing. Do not reach. Trust yourself, your own shape, your own confinement to the inherent geometry of this universe. Use special awareness. Remember timing. Count your beat."

Step, punch, low block, knife hand. Turn. Forearm forward block, side kick, back fist. Turn. Step, punch, low block—Gabriel practiced. Counted. Moved to the beat.

One and two, and one and two.

"Chin tucked, posture straight," she said.

"Yes, Mistress." Enough time had passed that calling her that was natural and didn't sound inappropriate. She was in charge and head of this facility. She made it clear early on challenging her on her authority would be a bad idea. And if these past months of discipline had taught Gabriel anything, it was she knew what she was doing and, slowly, so did he.

Learn. Concentrate. Focus. The future will come in its own time. Live here. Live now. To do otherwise and worry about Winnipeg or Redsaw or even what happened after Valerie— sorrow seized him and he stopped mid strike and lowered his arm. A small trickle of tears ran down from the corner of each eye.

"Gabriel?" she said. He had expected her to yell at him.

He looked over then wiped his eyes with his sleeve. "I'm sorry, Mistress. It won't happen again."

Her face was stern and her eyes cold . . . then those green emeralds softened and so did her expression. She came up to him and put a hand on his shoulder. When she spoke, it was softly. "The world did come to an end, didn't it?"

All he could do was nod.

She remained silent. "I know what that is like."

He glanced at her.

"I have not told you where I come from, but now you are ready to hear the truth."

Truth? "What . . . truth?"

"I am from five thousand years in the future. The earth was at war at the End of Time. The battle was to conclude history. But it carried on when it wasn't supposed to. And, after, so did the world. I am from here, this land and area, but from another time."

It sounded crazy, but he had seen enough with the black clouds and himself winding up in the past and fighting alongside the Crimson Cloak that believing her seemed the only option. It would explain her skill because her martial art was on a level he had never seen before in his era. She seemed to act and speak in a way that was foreign and, to a degree, not current either. Except, it wasn't her that wasn't current.

It was him.

If she was telling the truth.

"How did you—"

"Get here?" she said.

"Yes." The word barely came out.

"By force."

"By force?"

She looked down, did a subtle shake of the head, then looked him in the eye. "You need to trust me, Gabriel. If this is to work, you have to do as I say."

She lost him. "For what to work?"

"Please, trust me. I have not led you astray thus far, and I do not mean to as we go forward. Do you understand?"

There was no option here. He had come too far. He could not leave. He could not be apprised of what was happening in the city. He was not allowed to learn what Redsaw was doing at this very moment. It was either follow the program or . . . or . . . he didn't know what. She'd kill him? He doubted it. But she was right. She had not steered him wrong so far. Objectively, there was only one choice: Obey.

"Yes, Mistress," he said. "I understand."

She gave his shoulder a small squeeze and it was then Gabriel knew she cared. Whether about him or just simply about training someone, he didn't know, but for now, he'd take what he could get. "Time to go back to work," she said.

He nodded.

She stepped off to the side, waited a moment, then said, "Resume."

———

The month of doing forms set the movements in stone or, at least, what was acceptable enough for Aiyesha right now. Gabriel hoped it was enough. Knowing her, if she was dissatisfied, she'd bring it upon him unawares and get him to put in another month of forms.

Gabriel stood in the ready position on the outer rim of the mat.

"Fighting is multi-dimensional. It is not linear nor a strict method of straight back and forth. It is also not even simply getting tossed off to the side. It occurs on all sides, all angles, up, down, left, right, and everything in between. You must project a sphere around you for this is your combat zone. Your ideal is to keep the sphere small, but you also must allow it to expand if needed. Do you understand?"

"Yes, Mistress."

"Good. You will bring up your guard and move in a circle around the edges of this mat. When I say, you will step six feet inward and do it again. And when I say again, you will step in another six feet, ultimately arriving at the nucleus of your circle, your zone in which to keep the fight. But you also must be aware of the outer sphere. Do you understand?"

"Yes, Mistress."

"You will move opposite your strength and circle to the left. For the next twelve hours, you will circle to the left. You will begin . . . now."

Gabriel brought up his guard and began side-skipping sideways, trying to find a rhythm of which to follow. Once he found his stride, he kept moving left, enjoying the reprieve from the constant forms and *set* ways of executing a technique.

This is easy, he thought. *For now. You have another twelve hours ahead of you and already you're starting to feel the strain on the left. Let's hope it gets easier the tighter the circle.* No matter how he looked at it, he was grateful for this effort to grow strength on his left side, his weaker side. Not when he was Axiom-man, but just when being himself.

He kept the circle, still maintaining the outer rim. He wondered when she'd call him closer, but instead Aiyesha merely stood there, arms crossed, watching him.

"Mind your feet," she said as he passed by. "Do not lose control of your ankle. Find a rhythm between your own effort and control and momentum. Find the balance."

He nodded and noticed his guard had dropped a little. He immediately brought it back up, not wanting to catch heck.

To the left.

———

Five days.

Five whole long stinking days of circles. Day one was to the left. Day two to the right. Day three was to the left again. Day four was to the right. On day five, Aiyesha called out which direction and he had to change movement on the spot.

He was instructed to envision an opponent at the center of the mat. "But not Redsaw or anyone real. Imagine an opponent that frightens you." It varied throughout the day. Sometimes it was someone large, grizzly and tough as nails. Other times it was a mere common crook. The point of the exercise was to circle in closer and closer to your target. Boy, had he been wrong about the circling getting easier the closer you moved in. He had to shorten his stride and use other muscles to contain the contracted effort.

Dizziness.

Fatigue.

All common from circling, she'd told him, but during day five, Gabriel noticed he was called inward toward the center of the mat often. It appeared the main effort was to keep the circle small but still be aware of larger expansion if needed. In the end, muscle memory began to set in and each movement to the right or left became more natural.

As he lay on his cot on rest day, he was instructed to mentally review, ponder, and reflect on all he'd learned thus far. She said the visualization exercise would help his conscious mind to absorb and truly soak in all it could and then, as she explained it, allow the run-over to flow into his subconscious for processing and memory.

"Though you fight from the heart, the body obeys the mind therefore you must teach it to act precisely as you instruct it."

The room was dark, quiet, the air still. The idea was to remove external stimulation to help with a complete recovery. Between bouts of ponderance and sleep, he ate whole food meals, foods rightly divided and prepared for him by Aiyesha. He couldn't picture her in a kitchen—if there was a kitchen in this place—cooking up a storm. Whatever procedure was in place, Aiyesha took care of his nutritional needs.

As he lay in the dark, for some reason that coffin when he first arrived entered his mind. In hindsight, there was a moment upon waking when the thought entered his mind that everyone thought he'd died and he'd been buried alive by accident.

That would have been impossible, he thought. *The body is drained before burial.* Then it hit him. *Unless you're me. I doubt any draining of my body would have been permitted, and since Aiyesha and Katie somehow got a hold of me and brought me here, they wouldn't have allowed another soul to come near me. Whoever would have tried would have been destroyed in the attempt.* It didn't matter now anyway. He wasn't dead. If anything, he was more alive now than he had been in a long time.

Left. Left. Left. Left. The circle.

Right. Right. Right.

Left. Left. Right. Left.

Right. Right. Left. Right.

Around and around.

Around.

———

The next day, Gabriel was up early as his internal clock was now programmed to do . . . except Aiyesha never came to his door. Puzzled, he slowly rose from his cot, did a quick stretch, bent over, touched his toes, then grabbed behind his ankles and slowly drew his torso closer to his legs for a good lower back and hamstring stretch. He couldn't kiss his knees, but with all the stretching prior to training, he was much more flexible now than he had ever been even when he had his powers.

"Flexibility leads to dexterity. Dexterity leads to precision and timing. Precision and timing lead to victory," Aiyesha had said.

He appreciated how she instructed. Despite many items being required to do a technique on demand, she always explained why a certain technique or a certain exercise was done a specific way. Not only was she simply looking out to avoid injury that would set them back, she gave him the rules of the human body and how it reacted under various stresses, whether that was lifting weights or executing a technique.

As he walked to the door, already he pictured the combat sphere around him, his mind and body tracking his surroundings.

Spider sense, he thought with a wry grin.

Gabriel went down the hallway and headed toward the main facility. When he entered, the lights were already on and the mat clear save for a small dark brown, polished wooden table with a circular top. He walked over to it and found his breakfast along with a note.

The eggs, sausage, and rustic whole grain toast with olive oil were room temperature, Aiyesha no doubt not giving him a hot meal on purpose. He knew by now it was to keep him humble, to teach him not everything in life was handed to you perfectly, and sometimes you had to eat something that wasn't all that great. He knew all this just from everyday life but doing so every single day was a different animal. Still, he understood and embraced it.

TRANSFORMATIONS

A folded note lay beside the dish, a room-temperature smoothie beside it. Gabriel opened the note and read:

Today you will do what your generation terms "shadow boxing." In your case, it is termed, "shadow kickboxing." While you know the fundamentals of Muay Thai, this is not what that term is referring to. He had already figured that part out. *Today you will practice your sphere against an imaginary opponent. This opponent, like the others of your mind, will not be anyone you know and is to be fictitious. Stay focused. Upon practice, it is the same as using the heavy bag but without the bag. Strike fast, strike hard, but not full power otherwise you will risk injury hitting the air as hard as you can. Three-quarter power is sufficient for this exercise.*

I will not supervise, for your goal today is to practice your combinations in five-minute rounds. I have left a timer on the table. Gabriel glanced to it. It was an old winding watch. At least, that's what it looked like. He could figure out how to use it. How it would let him know his five minutes was up, he wasn't sure. But he trusted her.

Your purpose in this is as follows:

My being absent will allow you the ease of thought on observing how you move and which techniques you use. Be mindful of repetition and always defaulting to a favorite combination. Stop yourself when this occurs. I say "when" because you do have patterns and those patterns need breaking. You must always keep your opponent uncertain as to your next effort. This is not to say you must consciously do a wild variety of techniques or practice every single thing you have been taught. In combat, you do not use everything you know. You only use what is necessary.

This exercise is your self-discovery. Find your rhythm and your style. Take your time as you start your rounds. Begin casually. Work on improvisation. Work on observing what you do subconsciously and what you do consciously. Harmonize the two.

Those who follow the martial way do not go into every battle the same way, whether that battle is small or large. Each practitioner has their own style and method. Finding yours will eventually determine your effectiveness on the battlefield. Take the time to learn, Gabriel. This particular exercise is about you finding you.

Remember, start slow. Five-minute rounds. Watch your breathing. Watch your technique. Listen to yourself and flow with the combination that comes forth. After execution, reflect if it would have been effective or not. Then repeat.

I will come later to review.

She didn't sign her name; not that he expected her to. Did they even have personal signatures in the—he still had a slightly hard time with it. Relatively immediate timeline travel he understood, but five thousand years ahead? That was quite the distance along space-time. And that battle she spoke of? She didn't say when it would occur only that it had.

He just hoped he wasn't somehow involved somewhere down the line because that battle, as Aiyesha had said, happened at the End of Time.

He stood staring at the paper for a moment then snapped himself out of his rumination.

Gabriel set the paper down and began breakfast.

He had work to do.

As he chewed the lukewarm food—the eggs had started to become rubber—he eyed the center of the mat. At first, it was just a blank space, but soon it filled with the image of a large man standing seven-feet tall and weighing a solid three hundred pounds most of which was muscle. Gabriel opted to envision a wildly stronger opponent on purpose because Aiyesha taught him that strength had nothing to do with size and muscle.

At first, he couldn't reconcile the difference between the strength he gained in the gym and the power he gained through practice. But yesterday while resting, he finally understood the point: his strength training enabled his body to move and do what he commanded it to do. The power training through foundational techniques and forms was now able to flow through a body that could handle it and do whatever was asked of it.

"To use an item of your era," Aiyesha had said, "imagine your body as a full water hose." She stopped. "That is a ridiculous label, by the way, but as is where your civilization is at on the timeline, such juvenile terms are to be expected." The comment was harsh but she wasn't wrong. "This hose is full because you have turned on its water source. However, it is your choice when to release the water within depending on the intended purpose. I will spell out the metaphor so there is no confusion: The hose is powered and ready to be used when activated. You are the same. Fluid and malleable yet firm like the hose, but upon execution of your techniques, the hose is turned on. Once the technique is complete, the hose is turned off. When the hose is on, a portion becomes rigid due to the force of the water within. It becomes softer when it is off despite the water still being there. This is how you will fight."

She did an okay job of explaining it and he didn't fault her for awkwardly talking about an unfamiliar item. If she had used an example from her time, he likely wouldn't have understood it.

Swallowing the last bit of dry toast and washing it down with the remainder of his protein-infused smoothie, Gabriel stood, allowed a moment for his stomach to settle, then stepped onto the mat.

His opponent waited for him. The large man didn't move.

Gabriel found his distance, brought up his guard, and set his thoughts on task. He shifted his weight to the balls of his feet and concentrated on remaining on his toes.

The circle began.

He began with light jabs, a tease to his opponent and something, he hoped, would cause it to react, whether physically or mentally. After a few jabs, he followed through with a straight punch with his right then followed it up with an expedient shot from his left.

He worked his way in a circular pattern around his opponent, taking it slow as his mistress instructed. While this was no different than working the heavy bag, it was different in that he imagined a person instead of looking at a simple bag of sand.

He drew back, kicked, spun with a reverse crescent then launched in with a double punch to the midsection.

His breathing had been correct for a long time now and was close to second nature, but he remained mindful of it.

Punch. Punch. Kick. Knee.

Elbow. Elbow. Knee. Downward punch to an imaginary back of the head.

Soon, he would have his opponent retaliate, and he would work from that.

It had been four hours and no sign of Aiyesha. A large clay pitcher of iced green tea without sweetener by the foot of the round table kept his thirst at bay.

Soaked with sweat, he kept going, kept moving, his techniques coming faster and faster and more instinctual as he found his groove. As instructed, he watched for obvious repetition and even went a step further to see if there was repetition that was less obvious.

When he tired, he'd either lightly bounce on the spot to maintain light feet, or he'd practice quick circles to the right or left, both longer strides and short, both inward and outward, making sure he kept moving around his opponent.

He was so used to Aiyesha watching his every move that even during that first hour, he couldn't help but sense eyes were on him. He chalked it up to paranoia based on history and when Aiyesha never showed herself starting the second hour, Gabriel began to loosen up and really focus on himself and take his time. He ensured he remained active during those five-minute rounds, but he spent the one-minute rest time in between conducting very slow movements of his hands and feet. He purposefully moved slowly to analyze technique, how it felt, what seemed more natural versus other maneuvers.

Two and a half hours after, he was still at it. Two and a half hours after that, he was at it still. The large pitcher of iced tea had been emptied about a half hour back. Gabriel glanced around the room for another water source but found none. He wasn't concerned. There was enough liquid in his body that he'd be just fine even if he got thirsty. True, he was drenched in sweat head to toe, but that volume of water had been replaced by the iced tea. Perhaps that was why he didn't feel the need to use the bathroom and instead was able to focus on training and training alone.

When the twelve hours were up, limbs weak and rubbery, he shuffled to the table and picked up her note and re-read it, wanting to make sure he hadn't forgotten anything.

He hadn't. He had completed the day.

Back at his room, a small note was on his pillow.

It read: *Tomorrow. Repeat.*

He put the note down on the floor and sat on the edge of his bed. Here alone, it sometimes got tough, when his head wasn't so focused on and full of training. Thoughts of Winnipeg in ashes went through his mind. Thoughts of Valerie burning. Thoughts of Redsaw having absolute power. But he wasn't to go there. He was to keep present, let those items go, focus on what he was doing.

Aiyesha had told him from the start that each and every thing she had him do was for a reason. She had proven herself as someone capable, confident, knowledgeable, and wise. He had to trust she knew what she was doing on all fronts.

He had to.

Chapter Ten

Night.

Gabriel awoke, something not right. He eyed the dark, and a few moments later when he fully came around, he listened.

He wasn't alone.

He didn't hear any movement nor breathing, but something—someone—was inside his sphere.

"Mistress?" he said quietly.

In an instant, he was removed from his cot, pulled upright, received a hard shot to the head; it felt like a foot but he could have been mistaken. Then a sharp torquing of his shoulder and arm as he was forced to bend at the waist, arm behind his back in a chicken wing, a firm grip around his wrist with another point of pressure pushing up on his elbow, making it hurt even more.

"Do not react when taking a blow," he had been instructed as Aiyesha gave him points to ponder while he had circled the room.

Gabriel kept the pain inward, but before he could attempt an escape, he was sent to the floor, received a stomp with a heel against his solar plexus, immediately taking the air out of him and causing his guts to lock up in pain.

The door never opened, but he knew he was suddenly alone.

Why Aiyesha attacked him in his sleep, he didn't know. Worse, he hadn't been ready for it. Hadn't even countered. She got him so fast there wasn't even time to react.

His stomach sank. All that training and for what?

As he crawled back onto the cot, he had to remind himself to trust her.

————

When Gabriel awoke, the first thing his eyes set their sight on was the crack in the door. It wasn't open last night. That door had remained closed the whole time, even when Aiyesha attacked him. Was this just her way of getting him out of bed today?

He sat up, swung his legs over to the side of the cot and put his face in his hands. He pulled his fingers away because his thumbs were getting tangled in his beard. He ran a hand over his head, pushing back hair that had gotten far too long. It seemed grooming wasn't a priority here.

He stood and made his way to the door, not bothering with the light switch. The light from the hallway beyond was illumination enough. In the hallway, Gabriel peered left then right. No one was there. Not that he expected Aiyesha standing outside his door with wide open arms for a morning hug.

As he walked toward the facility, that strange feeling he was being watched came over him again, its presence entering his sphere. He checked around and found no one. At the facility door, he looked behind himself one more time.

He was alone.

Gabriel entered. The room was empty. So was the mat. All had been tidied, and it felt like if he moved something, he'd get in trouble for setting it out of place. He went over to the table for his breakfast but found only a smoothie. He supposed it'd have to be enough. Perhaps breakfast was after whatever would happen next?

The smoothie went down with ease, filling his eager stomach. He was hungry and hoped as the smoothie settled, he'd feel more satiated.

He stepped into the center of the mat and assumed the ready position. Each side of the room was empty save the equipment. He looked up, down, behind. Just him. So he waited.

To pass the time, he cleared his mind and reviewed as much as he could, starting with the basics and working his way up to the more complicated techniques. The room faded from view and all he saw were striking fists and feet, grabs and pulls, trips and throw-downs. He had to admit his ground game was weak. Aiyesha hadn't gotten into those techniques with him just yet.

"In an encounter, you must do all you can to remain standing. If it goes to the ground, so be it, but the moment you are able to stand, do so. But don't let the other person get up," she'd said.

From his left, something dark appeared. He remained ready in case this was a test from Aiyesha. Face forward, he peeked to his right. As the figure came more into view, his heart lightened.

Katie.

She wore her Night Fowler uniform, face covered.

Gabriel set his eyes forward and waited. When she stood in front of him, he said, "Katie? Where have you been? I wondered . . ."

She gracefully brought her arms into a guard and set her footing.

"Katie? What are you doing?" he asked.

She didn't move.

"Today, Gabriel," Aiyesha said, stepping onto the mat. He hadn't heard her enter. He never heard her enter nor her footfalls when she walked. "Today you will begin to put into practice all that we've covered thus far. Night Fowler will be your teacher. Together, you will spar. The aim right now is not to take the other person down. The aim is to learn. I want your speed, your technique, your power . . . but your power drawn back so we can practice engagement."

"Yes, Mistress," he said not taking his eyes off Kat—Night Fowler.

Aiyesha came and stood to the side but between them. "You will engage in combat and only cease when I say. Understood?"

"Yes, Mistress," they both said.

Hearing Katie say it gave Gabriel pause then, like a flood, everything fell into place. This was where Katie had gone after she disappeared. Or, at least, somehow wound up crossing paths with Aiyesha. Katie was already a formidable fighter when he met her and had skills he had never seen before. Aiyesha must have found her . . . or the other way around. Either way, Aiyesha was Katie's mistress, too.

"Begin," Aiyesha said softly, stepping away.

Night Fowler shot out a fist and clipped Gabriel along the jaw. He took the blow. He was so surprised she'd hit him, there was no other reaction.

Aiyesha raised a hand. "Stop." She stepped between them and stood directly in front of Gabriel. "Are you blind? Her shoulder moved. Why did you just stand there?"

"She's a girl," he said.

"No," Aiyesha said, "this is Night Fowler. A warrior, and you will treat her as such. Understood?"

He nodded.

"I said, understood?"

He nodded again. "Yes, Mistress."

"Again." To Katie, "Night Fowler."

"Yes, Mistress," she replied.

Gabriel set his guard, remembered his breathing and got ready.

"Remember to relax," Aiyesha told him. "Let it come naturally. Don't fight. Don't overthink. Don't obsess over technique and technical execution. The technique has been set in you for a long time. It's there. Trust it. Use it." She nodded in Night Fowler's direction. "Fight her."

Gabriel settled into his guard, made a conscious effort to relax and did his best to put out of his mind he was about to fight Katie.

"No fear," Aiyesha said. "Don't presume. Just react." She nodded at Night Fowler.

Immediately, Night Fowler went on the attack, shooting out her leg. Gabriel knocked it down with a low block before kicking out the same way. Night Fowler moved to the side and he missed. She came in with a fist from the side, tagging Gabriel in the side of the head. He glanced at Aiyesha. Her expression was unreadable nor could be given a label. She just looked at him as if staring at a wall.

"If you mind her, you will lose me," Night Fowler said.

"Right," Gabriel said, resetting his guard.

"Try again, Gabriel," Night Fowler said. "She's taught you. Use it."

He took a deep breathe, exhaled, waited a moment, then launched a backfist followed by a hook with the same hand. Night Fowler ducked on both and shoved him away in the chest.

"Keep moving," Night Fowler said. "Your sphere. The circle. Don't stop."

He delivered a front kick followed by a turning kick with the other leg then landed the foot and set forth a double punch twice with each hand. Night Fowler blocked each blow but there seemed to be a cooperation in it. Maybe she was part of his program too, and it was her turn to teach.

She sent a crescent kick toward his head. He blocked with an outer forearm block then tried a push kick but fell woefully short when she stepped back. He lunged forward from the effort but quickly straightened himself and got his guard back in place.

"Good," Night Fowler said.

Gabriel poured on the punches, doing his best to mind his technique all the while reacting as Aiyesha had instructed.

"Find yourself, Gabriel," Aiyesha said. "Find your way. You have the knowledge and the capability. You now need to let yourself express it in whatever manner it manifests. Let it happen. Your mind, body, spirit all know what to do. Let. Go."

Gabriel forwarded a side kick followed by a reverse side kick then a jumping elbow down on his target. Night Fowler moved at the last microsecond but he was fairly certain he would've gotten her with that last one if she hadn't.

She kicked. He blocked. He kicked. She blocked. The rhythm from the forms started to make sense.

One and two, and one and two.

"Exert your power, Gabriel!" Aiyesha shouted.

Gabriel eyed Night Fowler, his eyes now no more than cold as stone. She moved in. He blocked, ran his hand down her arm to the elbow, exerted pressure, spun her and shoved her away. He was in the air without thinking. "Ayah!" A flying side kick landed right in Night

Flower's middle. She hop-skipped with the blow, but the point had been made.

He had got her.

———

After four days of strict sparring with Night Fowler, Gabriel began to understand what Aiyesha meant when she said to let go. Not only did the sparring serve as combat practice, it was also an exercise in self-mastery and self-relaxation. Gabriel just wished the relaxation part involved actual relaxation and not merely settling into oneself and one's current combat style. Regardless, the relaxation worked. Aiyesha only corrected him when something obvious went wrong, like when Night Fowler clocked him twice on each side of the head with a hook to the right and the left, rocking his world despite her holding back. Aiyesha explained how to avoid it next time, whether through offense or defense. He made an effort to absorb all he could and did his best to put it into practice despite sometimes clumsy efforts.

Today was different. Today the program finally changed. Sort of.

Today was about reactionary sparring.

"What do you mean by reaction?" Gabriel asked Aiyesha.

"It is a simple exercise meant to build intuition, discernment, and reflex. The process is simple, Gabriel. You strike. She strikes. One for one. Back and forth, acceleration of exchange is your goal as you learn and go along. Whatever she sends your way, react with something of your own from the position you are in. Choose your target yet be quick about it. Just . . . react."

"Understood," he said. "Um, understood, *Mistress.*" She seemed more pleased with that response than the other.

He squared up against Night Fowler and set his guard. She did the same.

"Begin when you're ready," Aiyesha said.

Gabriel had hoped for an official ringing of the bell, but instead had to remain in anticipation for what might come next. Should he strike first? Should she? What was better to start off with? Defense? Offense? He didn't know the rules yet also understood from experience that real-life combat didn't have any rules.

Night Fowler threw light jabs over and over, clearly trying to get him focused on them and distracted for the real blow to follow.

Gabriel moved in with a quick turning kick to Night Fowler's side. She blocked him but that wasn't the point at the moment. A front kick came at him. He moved in for a straight punch. A side kick from her sent him backward and gained her some distance. Gabriel returned the same technique but covered his distance with a slide first then put out the kick. A punch from her. A kick from him. A kick from her. A reverse side kick from him. A forward straight punch. Gabriel raised his front leg and sent a hooking kick to her head. She ducked as he grazed the top of her hood. She dove in with a punch to his chest. Coughing, Gabriel looked to Aiyesha. This was supposed to be partial power, not full, unless Night Fowler was able to strike so hard this *was* her partial power. Aiyesha merely pointed in Night Fowler's direction. She closed in despite it being his turn to throw a strike. He did a jumping front kick. Night Fowler moved to the side and went for a low kick to his knee. Gabriel returned the same.

TRANSFORMATIONS

Back and forth.
Back and forth.

———

Three weeks later.

The iron weights were gone, and Gabriel was allowed to do his strength training in the main facility, but despite it being equipped with its own traditional gym, he was to touch none of the equipment. This month, he was told, all resistance training would be using his body only. Besides some push ups or chin ups, he didn't know what else there was but, of course, Aiyesha showed him otherwise.

She outlined his routine and then he got to work.

Shoulder-width push ups. Two sets on his knuckles until failure. Two sets on his fingertips until failure.

Chin ups. Two sets should-width, elbows in tight. Two sets wide grip.

Squats. Bodyweight for warmup until the burn was unbearable then, on rubbery legs, one-legged squats— which took a little practice to get the coordination and balance right—followed by walking lunges.

Short break spent bouncing on his toes and moving in a tight circle.

Fingers locked together, one palm up, one palm down, mid-chest, every effort made to work against himself to try and pull his hands apart. Isometrics.

Palm presses in which he pushed his hands together as hard as he could and had to hold the position.

One-legged, bicep pull ups with both hands cradling one foot while standing on one leg, the foot in his hands pressing down while he pulled forward in a curling motion. He was to maintain the pressure against his hands but allow his arms to perform the movement.

Sit ups and leg raises.

Back bends and raises.

Twists.

The hardest were inverted push ups. It was the same as a barbell shoulder press except he was upside down, back against the wall while he faced outward standing on his hands. Aiyesha kept a palm to his ankles to start, preventing his legs from toppling forward and disengaging the exercise. Gabriel lowered himself then pressed against the ground, doing his best to forget he was upside down and aimed at control of his body, keeping it straight, while he moved up and down.

The body was worked in full three days a week with a rest day in between. On the days there was no strength training, he was shadow kickboxing, running the track, skipping rope and running through all fourteen forms he knew as cool down. All under Aiyesha's strict supervision.

"It is best to do your forms first then your strength training to prevent accidental poor form. However, as part of the Acceleration, you will perform them last, for in combat, fatigue can come and yet you still have to fight. Concentrate and master your limbs, Gabriel. Mind over body, heart over mind."

She had been right about the potential for sloppy technique because doing that first walking punch as part of Form A made him realize he did have to buckle down on the control thanks to sluggish limbs from working out.

Gabriel practiced.

————

TRANSFORMATIONS

Time stopped. Without access to the outside world, all Gabriel had to go on was his internal body clock but even that could have gotten screwed up from waking in that coffin. The only way to measure the passing time was counting workouts, but even that was unreliable because it wasn't always train all day, stop, sleep, wake, train, stop, sleep . . . . As time went on, Aiyesha seemed to have made it a habit to get him from his room at any moment. Sometimes it felt like he had gotten a mere few hours of sleep, other times a full night's worth, and the duration of the sessions was not based on how much sleep he got.

Aiyesha began each summoning the same way: "You must be ready at any moment. Come, I want to show you something." And then would proceed teaching him a focused lesson or a review of lessons. He'd cool down, have a shower, return to his room, think about what they studied to hopefully feed the information into his subconscious for permanent residence, then rest, only for him to soon hear, "You must be ready at any moment."

Gabriel lay on his cot, letting go of his body and allowing it to become dead weight. Each part, each limb, all of him. As his eyes closed, he was ready for Aiyesha to show and say . . . "You must be ready."

You must be ready.
You must be ready.

CHAPTER ELEVEN

THE ROOM WAS dimly lit, the large candle lamps hanging from the ceiling provided a cone of illumination on the wooden floor, but everything outside that cone's diameter was shadow. She was in here with him, but Gabriel didn't know where. Night Fowler never made a sound when she moved. Never took an audible breath. Thankfully, Gabriel had the same advantage. The past several months were spent on punching and kicking drills, repeating techniques and forms ad nauseum, and plenty of sparring with Night Fowler, everything from purposeful non-contact where your strike would land an inch from target, to reactionary sparring, to partial power and, sometimes, full power, no holding back.

"You get hit, you keep moving. It didn't happen. Take it and move," Aiyesha had told him. "There is no excuse to not move after receiving one or more strikes. The only excuse is death or being unconscious." It was harsh, but that drive, that determination, that will to stand after getting knocked down was something Gabriel kept in the fore of his mind. He tried not to think of how that maybe cost him the city. Cost him Valerie. Cost him everything. All he could do right now was remain present-minded and stay on task. He wasn't sure if he was earning his stripes with powers waiting at the end, or if this was his calling now and he was to be like Night Fowler—without ultra powers but fully capable to stop evil nonetheless.

Gabriel peered around the corner of one of the multiple seven-foot-square wooden crates in the room. What was in them, if anything, he didn't know.

She was around here somewhere, and he had to find her.

Cautiously, he moved around the crate, guard at the ready, feet light. He kept his sphere on alert, searching for any sound or indication of movement. He eyed the halos of light on the floor, searching for a shadow. Night Fowler was too smart for that. She had learned how to remain invisible from Aiyesha, and Gabriel was only learning now. This was another lesson.

He quickly glanced up then back down in front of him. He rounded the crate, remaining in its shadow. The next crate was roughly ten feet away. To get over to it, he'd have to move quickly, try and stay outside the halo of light and not let a drip of his shadow skitter across the floor and tip Night Fowler off.

Gabriel kept his back to the crate and notated his path: quick curve around the side of the crate he was up against, then a long stride with a fold of the leg into a soft roll then back to his feet against the other crate.

It seemed simple enough and he was capable of doing it. Aiyesha had already sent him through the rungs of basic gymnastics.

Keeping his breathing silent, knowing that fluidity without hesitation was key, Gabriel minded his guard and set his foot out. As fast as he could, he leaned over his leg, collapsed it beneath him, quickly rolled along the ground, then stood, back to another crate, guard up.

"Hi," Night Fowler said. She was right beside him. Next thing Gabriel knew, he was slammed up against the crate, her forearm pressed against his throat. The more upward she pressed, the more he noticed himself rise on his tiptoes.

Gabriel brought his own forearm into the crux of her elbow, pressed forward and folded her arm against her, twisting with his back to her to deliver a reverse elbow to her head. She blocked it, sent a kick just as he faced her. He knocked it down, did a turning kick with each leg—one to her head, one to her middle. He scored the second shot then took a straight punch to the nose. His eyes watered but through the blur, he saw her gray shadowy form. He moved to jab for a feint. She took his wrist and yanked him forward, bringing him over and bending him at the waist.

"Where your head goes, your body goes," Aiyesha had told him a long time ago.

He kept his head upright as best as able and straightened his torso as far as he could against her. At the same time, he had his right hand formed as a claw and searched out her hamstring through her thick leggings. He found it, squeezed—the Horse Pinch—then scooped that leg out from under her, sending her backward. Night Fowler threw her arms back and did two back handsprings and disappeared into the dark.

You made it. Or she let you win. Either way, you're figuring this out, he told himself.

A creak came from off to the side. That was too obvious and definitely meant for distraction. Perhaps part of this exercise was to block out the inessentials and maintain focus on what needed to be done?

He circled through the dark, minding the crates, keeping away from the direction of the creak.

Unless that's what she wanted.

It started to sink in that maintaining distance and keeping out of sight wasn't just an issue of planning and patience, but also a psychological game so your opponent would never see you coming.

His legs went out from underneath him with a violent tug. He sprung back onto his feet, guard up, searched the dark.

Stop toying with me, he thought. He crept through the shadows. Coming up to another corner of a crate, something didn't sit right within his sphere.

There was only one way to find out if his senses were indeed sharpening.

He neared the corner, shifted his weight to his back leg, then did a frontward reverse turning kick, his heel hitting pay dirt when he knocked her in the chest as she stayed against the adjacent wall of the crate. The weird thought of hitting a woman in the chest flashed through his mind then disappeared just as quickly. She had armor. It was clear by her build in uniform, which was why he couldn't distinguish her from a male when he first laid eyes on the Night Fowler.

She quickly rounded the crate to where he was, hook swinging. He ducked; she pulled it and went for an shovel hook to his gut. He blocked it down, kicked forward, spun with an axe kick. His heel came down on her shoulder the second she brought in a crescent kick with the other leg. Her foot swept across his jaw, sending his head to the side. He moved with the blow as taught then looked back her way.

She was gone.

He needed more practice.

———

Gabriel presumed it was approximately two months later. He still had no way to tell.

The wing chun dummy stood before him. Forearms crashed against wooden poles as he furiously executed blocks and strikes against it, incorporating foot and knee techniques to the wooden leg that protruded from its center.

Triple punch. Forearm left, forearm right, low, high, punch, punch, knife hand strike, elbow, block, block, high punch, low punch, kick, knee, kick, trip, high hooking kick, punch, punch, punch, faster and faster until his arms were a blur and he let muscle memory and instinct take over.

Faster.

Faster.

"Faster!"

———

Aiyesha sat cross-legged on the mat, forearms on her knees, palms up but hands relaxed. Her eyes were closed. Gabriel waited at the edge of the mat for fear of disturbing her.

"Come. Sit," she said.

He walked onto the mat and sat in front of her.

"Do as I do," she said.

He folded his legs and took a quick study on how she had her arms then mimicked her.

"Close your eyes, back straight but body relaxed."

He took a deep breath and exhaled slowly, settling in as he closed his eyes and got his body right.

"Stare into the darkness of your mind. Do not let thoughts enter, thoughts of any kind."

Throughout his training, Gabriel got a fairly solid grasp of being present-minded while he worked. He did the same here, focused on the moment, focused on the nothing before his closed eyelids, focused on brushing aside any thought that entered his mind and sent it back into the void.

The room was quiet.

He had an urge to open his eyes a crack to see if she studied him, but he also knew to go against instruction would also reap reprimand so he kept them closed.

"Today, this moment, you will draw in all external training and the workings of your body and bring them inwards. Visualize. Your training is all over you, in your muscles, your tendons and joints, your mind. Your heart. All of it, its entirety, must now come inwards and settle into your spirit. This is the Integration. This is where you will bring to a close the groundwork you have been taught. You will not close off the knowledge nor ability. You are simply taking that groundwork and putting it where it belongs: in the core of your spirit. If you put it there, it will underlie all you do going forward and, like a garden, serve as rich soil in which you can now grow and hone your skill. You can now learn new techniques and new ways of thought. Lay down the earth and settle your garden. Be mindful of the seeds planted and the sprouts already growing. Do not stifle nor cover them. Lay them out, ensure the root is deep. As you do this, you will water that soil by bringing those things into your spirit." She took a deep breath in through her nose and exhaled slowly through slightly-parted lips. "Begin."

Gabriel wasn't one hundred percent sure what to do but he had an inkling as to what she meant. So much training, so much repetition, so much sweat. He let his senses run through his body, a consciousness of sorts that drifted through his limbs and torso and mind, one sensitized to what he felt. His arms were no longer his own, he realized. There was power there, skill, built-in movement and subconscious reaction capability. His legs, though folded right now, had strength and ability, kicking high, kicking low, and any range in between. The balls of his feet stood out, a prime striking tool. His neck felt secure and steady, his head a weapon of its own. Elbows, knees, palms, and fingers—this was a different body than the one he arrived with. A different body than one he had ever known, and it wasn't the benefits of pure exercise either. It was something else. Something had entered him, a kind of electric spark that triggered his baser instincts of survival and necessary combat. There was a surety in place now, one that led him to believe, with some more time, he could consciously or even subconsciously command his hands and feet, elbows and knees with efficiency, proficiency, and purpose.

An element of body control was in place, one that was dismissed despite used to having powers. He could control those and activate them and use them when needed. This was different. This was him meeting himself without powers, without blue energy, without capes, and . . . without the messenger.

He needed more work, this he knew, but it felt as if he had overcome the crest of a hill and, indeed, all that soil he had been pouring was finally beginning to settle and ready to nurture seeds and make them grow.

Aiyesha had changed him. Changed his mind, even his heart. He wasn't sure if he should be mad at the intrusion or grateful, but it became truly clear his mistress wasn't a merciless fighter but rather a fighter than knew how to channel martial arts into the betterment of soul and mind.

How to improve a life.

Gabriel sat in silence, dark before his eyes, breathing calmly and surely.

TRANSFORMATIONS

Time ticked on. He didn't know how long, but when he opened his eyes, Aiyesha was gone.

Chapter Twelve

THIRTEEN MONTHS LATER.

Night Fowler came in hard, her cape spinning around Gabriel in an attempt to distract him. He blocked her kick, spun and delivered a reverse side kick straight for her middle. It sent her a foot back but she jumped up in a high front kick aimed for under his chin. She caught him, sending his head back. A sharp pinch hit the back of his neck from the over-extension.

The time for light sparring had long been over. Months ago. Now it was for real so he could learn to deal with the threat and fear associated with confronting a highly-trained combatant.

Right now, despite all this time, Gabriel was still unsure about going the distance with Night Fowler. Going the distance meant he would fight her until one of them dropped. Everything he dished out came back at him, at minimum, threefold. But, if anything, the intense retaliation sped up his skills and reaction time.

But the fear was still there. He could deal with a thrice-powered-and-sped return, but he wasn't sure if she'd crank it to a ten if he pushed hard. That . . . Kat—Night Fowler enjoyed this. Enjoyed the fight. Enjoyed wreaking destruction on someone else. What made her that way had yet to be revealed. Gabriel could only suspect a long time with Aiyesha might have changed her. At the same time, the girl he met when he was disguised as "Mike" had already been a strong fighter so clearly had an intense warrior spirit. How or why that was birthed in her however long ago, he didn't know and there was no time here at the Central to catch up. Casual talk was forbidden. Nothing mattered but martial combat.

Gabriel straightened his head only to receive a fist to the nose . . . on the bridge, no less.

He knew she had held back. Any harder and she would have broken it.

He quickly used the outside of his thumbs to brush away the instinctive tears then brought his guard back up. Night Fowler simply circled slightly to the side, brought out her arms in her own styled guard of one hand in a knife position, the other, a fist partly back, body slightly turned, closed position, which meant their chests were facing opposite directions.

Gabriel sent forward a front kick, which she swept to the side. As she moved in, he brought down the opposite leg in an axe kick, landing it hard on her shoulder then the heel sliding down the side.

"Follow through," she said, not breaking a beat. "Basics. *Through* the target, not on it or at it."

"Stupid mistake."

"A stupid mistake could cost you your life. Be careful. I'm not gonna give you another chance."

Gabriel didn't respond nor give any facial reaction. He merely ensured his guard and settled into it, controlled his breathing and relaxed into position.

She punched—a double—one landing, the other Gabriel blocked. He flew in with an elbow to the neck, which she bent around, spinning him with a push to the shoulder. She sent a push kick into his lower back good and hard but not to break the spine, just enough to send him to the ground.

Gabriel hit the floor sprawling, then did a quick push-up, catching sight of her out of the corner of his eye. He swung his hand around in a backfist. She ducked so he came with an uppercut with the opposite hand, connecting under her chin, this time forcing her hooded head backward. He leapt into the air and did a flying side kick to the middle of her chest. She stumbled far back, was able to regain her footing, but it was too late. Gabriel was on his way with a sliding side kick for the follow-through. He struck pay dirt and put her to the ground. As Aiyesha instructed, he didn't stop until he knew his opponent was no longer a threat. The moment she hit the ground, her guard was up, catching another axe kick effort. Didn't matter; it was distraction. He wanted her hands busy because he collapsed that same leg onto her, making his knee go forward and put weight on her face. He then hit her half power once on either side of the head to illustrate his point.

He got off her, stood beside her, and extended his hand to help her up. She whirled her legs and slapped his hand out of the way with her foot and sprung onto her feet.

This wasn't over.

———

As time passed, Gabriel was called to combat at all hours, the simple lesson being death could come at any time. Some nights, he was so tired from training that pouncing off the bed and delivering strikes felt like a dream. Other times, the combat was so intense, a jolt of adrenaline woke him up and he was ready to rapid fire without issue.

He just wished he knew how long this would go on for. He'd been here at the Central for so long and had lost track of the days. A pit of heavy guilt settled in his stomach. Winnipeg, the city . . . there was no telling what was happening to it or even if it was still standing. He knew the outside world was being kept from him on purpose so he could remain focused under Aiyesha's tutelage. He just didn't expect it to last as long as it had.

As Night Fowler's fist came in in a tight and strong left hook, Gabriel ducked, gave two punches to each front deltoid, charlie-horsing the muscles. Night Fowler's arms dropped and her effort to bring her arms back up was feeble. It didn't seem to bother her, however, because he knew she had five other striking tools at her disposal, never mind what she might possibly know about using compromised limbs in combat. That was one lesson Gabriel would like to learn: how to fight when you couldn't move. Perhaps thisat was a lesson for somewhere down the line. Regardless, Night Fowler's feet came at him, the dexterity in her knees, legs, and ankles replacing her arms with the same efficiency.

A kick toward his head. Blocked.

A kick to the head from the other side. Blocked.

One toward his middle. Blocked.

She kicked his guard away with a partial crescent kick then a fully-powered side kick to his chest. He went flying back, hit the floor, brought up his knees, semi-loose, and put up his hands and arms in a low guard to dispel any chances of strikes to sensitive parts as well as the rest of him.

The kick came down. Gabriel knocked it away, rolled to the side so he faced the ground, pushed himself up, kicking sideways upon the ascent. He struck air but it was enough to get her to take a small step back to avoid it while he finished righting himself and came forward with a front kick followed by a spinning back kick. Night Fowler blocked the first kick with her knee but thanks to the rise of her leg, it left her like a flamingo, making scoring the second kick pretty simple.

What was incredible was her resiliency and seeming endless endurance.

"A fight can be over within a single blow, but generally speaking, they last thirty to forty-five seconds. Most people, the common person, does not have the endurance to last longer than that because they expel all their energy at the fore in an attempt to defeat their opponent quickly. If you last longer than that initial minute, Gabriel, you will be at a strong advantage over them because they will be weak and tired and you will still be strong and refreshed. This is why we run. This is why we put in the constant work. You may be just a man with all the limits of a man, but those limits can be extended and expanded to a significant degree. You cannot accept the finite abilities of your body despite training and give in to them. The human body is capable of miracles under the right circumstances. I am sure you have already heard of superhuman feats conducted by those without special abilities. I do not need to reiterate them, but they illustrate a single truth: the wall of human ability is more distant than you think. The question is, are you willing to travel to see how far away that wall really is? Because if you are, you will find your journey will be a long walk. And if walked correctly, the wall will always remain but you will never reach it because you will keep pushing it farther and farther away as you train. Understand?"

"Yes, Mistress," he had said.

"All you have been taught, all that you have learned, you must combine it all in expression. One can understand and be efficient and know every possible technique in terms knowledge, but applying those techniques in the right way at the right time is what separates decent fighters from great ones. I do not train decent fighters."

He could only hope she was implying he had surpassed being decent and was on a path to something better.

Back in the present, Night Fowler came in with a feigned punch then quickly wrapped her now-somewhat-useable arms behind his neck and over his shoulder. Her weight came down on him while she put a foot just behind his heel, forcing him backward off balance and to the ground. On top of him, she struck him in the side with her knee then brought that same knee down into his solar plexus. Sharp pain rocketed up from the spot and filled half his lungs and the upper portion of his gut with agony.

"If struck and breathing becomes difficult, you must relax and not panic despite instinct. Slow down. Small sips of air. Your lungs will hurt from wanting more oxygen, but you need to set it aside and focus on breathing otherwise panic might set in and you won't alleviate the urge to gulp air in a hurried effort for recovery." Aiyesha had been right in her statement because when she made him take a hard hit to the chest to get him to practice, it took all the mental fortitude he could muster to stay in the moment and focus on his breathing.

Now, he hoped, Night Fowler didn't notice that was what he was doing.

Slowly, thin breaths of air went into his lungs. Thin breaths of air went out.

Night Fowler's arms seemed to have recovered quickly or she was so good she knew how to override the feeble muscles. Her fist came to his face. He put up his guard but she punched through it, making regaining his breath much more difficult.

Still focusing on his breath, she came in for another strike to his head. Gabriel blocked her punch with his left forearm then used his right palm to press against the shoulder of her punching arm, folding the shoulder in and bringing her striking tool across her body. As he did so, he simultaneously sat up, rolling as he did, sending her over onto her back, him now on top. He delivered two quick sets of rapid double punches to her chest before putting a hand to her throat, the arc of his hand pressing hard against her trachea.

He raised his other fist. His legs pinned the tops of her thighs and forbade her hip flexors from moving, something needed if she was to attempt using her legs to get him off. He sunk as much of his weight as possible into her lower half, pinning her down.

"Yield," he said.

"I do not yield," she said.

Gabriel took a quick peripheral glance at how he had her immobilized. From what he could see, his position was secure.

"It seems you have two options, Gabriel," she said. "You can show mercy or you can grant judgement and hand out my sentence. Which will it be?"

I'm not going to choose. We're sparring. Obviously I'm not going to kill you. "This is practice," he said.

"Yes, but if it were not, what would you choose?"

The question should have been simple to answer. He was on the side of life, but he also knew from painfully endured experience one day he would likely make this call. He had wanted to kill Redsaw for what he did to Valerie, to the city, to him. Now, he didn't want Redsaw dead. He wanted him in perpetual torment.

"I don't know," he said.

"That is the correct answer," she said. "You do not know what you will do if under such a circumstance. It is one thing to train and discipline the mind, even the heart, but quite another to tame a warrior's spirit, the very spirit that drives your entire existence. It makes decisions for you. It makes you conduct certain thoughts and actions."

He still had his fist raised and her neck pinned down. "Then how will I know what the right choice is?"

"When it comes to choosing whether or not to kill, it is not a matter of right and wrong. It is a matter of if such an action is appropriate considering all factors, both large and extremely small. It is not up to us to end someone's days before their time no matter how horrible a person or crime they have committed. It is not for you to make that decision. However, there are times when that decision has to be made and, as is its nature, can only be made in that moment when all things are considered."

He absorbed her words in silence then rose off her.

She got to her feet and looked at him. All he could do was look back and be ready in case she decided to strike.

"It is complete. For now," she said. Night Fowler drew back her hood and let it settle on her shoulders and down her back. She reached up and slowly took off the mask. "It is time to go."

"Mistress?"

CHAPTER THIRTEEN

Gabriel had thought fighting Aiyesha would have been enough to demonstrate his ability, but like all things with her, it wasn't good enough and everything was subject to correction for perfection.

"As we sparred, I made note of that which still needs work. You have what you need, Gabriel. You have more than a foundation upon which to grow. Now it's time to refine what you know and smooth the wheel so you can be faster with more power behind each strike."

"I still cannot believe it was you, Mistress," he said.

"That is one area upon which you erred," she said. "Did you not notice a change in style? Did you not have sessions that were more difficult and challenging than others? One's fighting style is like a fingerprint. It is unique to all warriors despite how much they might try to mimic others."

"You mean—"

"It was not always me. It was also her. But you should have been mindful of the change in height and weight. You should have been mindful of how those factor into how a blow is delivered. You were not observant and that was the lesson."

"I'm sorry, Mistress." Now he mentally kicked himself.

"Merely keep it in mind for the future as it may provide a victory in an encounter."

"Yes, Mistress."

"Let us begin."

Gabriel got into the ready position.

"Show me how to make a proper fist," she said.

He held out his hand, palm open, then slowly folded his fingers inward, ensuring his thumb crossed his first two knuckles, his fist as square as a brick.

"Show me the striking position of the foot."

"For which kick?"

"All of them with names."

He nodded.

It was like starting from square one. Each day, as it was in the beginning, focused on a single technique, sometimes two, sometimes three. Instead of putting in long hours on a single strike or block, it was done through repetitions. Now adept at each technique, going through each movement one by one went along much quicker than before. He was to show her each specified technique at full speed and power, with her sometimes calling for him to slow it by half or a quarter or even push himself and speed it up by the same. Every time he erred, she'd put up her hand to stop him, came over, adjusted his hand or foot or leg even just a mere millimeter, then had him continue. If he messed up, she'd do it again.

This is getting annoying, he thought. It was almost time to leave. Deep inside, a thick yearning to get out of this building and get outdoors built hard and sure. It was as if he'd been in a densely crowded room for hours, hardly able to move, his body craving space and zero stimulation. But he knew that would only be possible if he finished his course.

Aiyesha was in charge, and she was the gatekeeper.

Gabriel punched again.

———

Aiyesha had her elbow wedged between where Gabriel's ribcage met in the middle, both of them on the ground. Each dig of the bone sent a sharp pain throughout his chest, stealing his breath. He took a swing at her. She blocked it with her free hand then gave a sharp press with the elbow again before getting up.

Coughing and trying to get some air, Gabriel got his feet under him. "How do I get out of that?"

Aiyesha seemed to consider the question with considerable thought. "That's a lesson for another time." She faced him squarely then eyed him up and down. Gabriel looked down at his feet to check what she looked at and when he straightened, Night Fowler was beside her. At least, he hoped it was the *real* Night Fowler.

Hoped it was Katie.

"*He's* ready," Night Fowler said.

A jolt shot through Gabriel's chest. The women had him so distracted with training he forgot the threat of encountering . . . *him*.

"No," Gabriel said. "I can't. I'm not ready. He'll kill me. Aiye—Mistress? Katie?"

"You will see him," Katie said. "Just as I had." She nodded toward Aiyesha. "Just as she had."

All this time. All this training. Was he even taught anything? Was it all some sort of elaborate method of fake fighting designed to convince him he still had something to offer. Could still be—

"He stole Valerie," Gabriel said firmly.

"Yes, he did," Aiyesha said. "What are you going to do about it?"

He wanted to say he was going to kill him but knew saying so would probably immediately lead him into the man's presence to be destroyed. Redsaw wouldn't care if he was powerless, wouldn't care if there was no ultra-powered fight. He'd just fire a blast of red energy into Gabriel and turn him to ash.

No amount of combat training would lead him to victory, at least, going toe-to-toe. And that seemed the only option right now. There was no time to plan, to think, to come up with some way to sneakily weaken Redsaw so he could take him on and, even if it was all fake fighting maneuvers, still somehow use the techniques to . . . to . . . Gabriel didn't know what. All he knew as the women approached him, he didn't have a choice.

Chapter Fourteen

As the three of them walked down a long hallway, out of his peripheral Gabriel took note of the doors on either side. Like the hallway near his room, they were not labeled, painted blue, no indication of what might lay beyond.

Aiyesha and Night Fowler walked on either side of him like a pair of escorting cops.

Heart picking up pace, Gabriel remembered his training and got to work on his breathing. In slow through the nose, out slow through the mouth. Silent. Calm.

Two opponents. One on either side. He went over his options. It'd have to be fast, hard, powerful. An aimed strike to each to somewhere soft and sensitive, something to get them to stop and have to either catch their breaths or at least double them over so he had enough time to sprint away.

Two doors were ahead, identical to the ones that led into the training facility. If they were indeed like the facility, and there was a room beyond and Redsaw was in it . . .

Gabriel went inward. He measured Aiyesha and Night Fowler up through the corner of his eyes. They would be fast on reaction, their training dictating their movements not they themselves.

Night Fowler's gear made discerning a weak spot difficult, but striking the target despite the uniform would be no different than striking through your opponent.

Don't let an outfit hinder you. You've been sparring with her— or Aiyesha in that suit—for months on end. It's a non-issue.

He had to take away their legs, get them on the ground without wrestling them down.

He could go for the "light posts" at the base of their skulls, but his aim would have to be bang-on for it to knock them out. If it worked, it would certainly stop the walking. If he missed or didn't hit hard enough, he'd merely be delaying a very dangerous fight, one that would likely result in his death unless that honor was reserved for Redsaw.

One choice.

One option.

It would be difficult but possible.

Aiyesha on his left, Night Fowler on his right, he got himself perfectly aligned between them so the three of them were in a perfect line.

Step, jump, and—Gabriel took to the air, bounding forward a few feet, his time in the air enough for them to take a step or two forward and walk into his strike. He shot out both legs, striking backward in a dual jumping back kick, heels aimed straight at their hip flexors. If he folded those, they would topple forward. Instead, a hand pressed on either shoulder blade, shoved him while in air, and sent him sprawling forward. He blocked his face with his forearms before he hit the ground, allowing them to absorb the shock with a slight bend before he rolled over, guard up, ready for whatever might come at him.

Both women stood over him. Night Fowler said, "Are you done?"

"I'm not going in there," he replied.

"Do not be afraid," Aiyesha said.

"What?" Gabriel said.

The dual doors opened behind him and a bright light filled the hallway. Both women immediately took an upright, formal posture, bowed, and said together, "Sir."

The light grew brighter as it grew closer. Gabriel spun on his back, guard still in place, ready for Redsaw to—

"Hello, Gabriel," the glowing man said. "I have a message for you."

It was the messenger.

———

The four were in a plain room, no décor nor decorations. No furniture or any other item that would indicate this was a used space. A skylight cast a bright glow into the room. Gabriel peered up through the glass, taking in the blue sky for the first time in he didn't know how long.

The messenger was now in the middle of the room, the women still on either side of him.

"I don't . . . I don't know what to say. Don't know what to think," Gabriel said softly.

"Go," Aiyesha said, her tone reassuring.

He glanced up at her, mind a complete muddle of confusion and theory as to what really had gone on here. Was this a trial? Was he in need of training and received it? Had the world gotten so bad out there the messenger was going to help somehow?

Aiyesha's normally stern expression softened and a slight hint of a smile rose at the corners of her eyes. She nodded.

Gabriel looked to Night—to Katie. She put a hand on his shoulder in reassurance then took it off just as quickly.

He looked to the messenger, who simply stood there, waiting, seeming to not be in any rush.

His heart picked up pace again. He had failed everyone, including the messenger. The idea it was now time for punishment sent his heartrate up even faster.

He drew his fingers into fists and assumed the ready position, channeling his power through his arms and *out* his fists in a mental push to send the anxiety away.

There was only one way to do this.

Gabriel bowed, held the low position a second longer than he normally would in an effort to demonstrate sincere peace and respect, then righted himself.

The messenger returned the bow with a slow nod of his head.

Gabriel exhaled and stepped forward. Instincts told him to get ready to fight, and while he appreciated the training to always be ready, he wouldn't have a prayer against the messenger no matter how skilled he might be.

"Sir," Gabriel said.

The messenger didn't react.

Gabriel thought for a moment. Nothing had come out of his mouth. He only thought he said the word. He tried to speak, to say it for real, but nothing would escape his lips.

"Leave us," the messenger told the ladies.

Gabriel didn't have to turn around to know they took a moment to bow before departing. He heard the dual doors close behind him.

The messenger's bright blue form was hard on the eyes. It was like staring into a bright blue-glowing sun. But he'd seen this before and somehow seeing this display of power contained within one man calmed him.

He knew him.

He'd known him ever since the night the messenger came and delivered unto him his powers. He just hoped the messenger was—Gabriel jolted his thoughts and realized he'd forgotten he had been so wrapped up in seeing Redsaw that seeing the messenger again . . . it'd been so long.

"It happened, didn't it?" the messenger said.

"I don't . . ."

"Your powers left you."

Gabriel nodded.

"You came here."

He nodded again. "I was in a box."

"You were dead. At least to the outside world."

"Dead?" He choked on the word. His heart had calmed but his legs went wobbly.

"Not in the truest sense." The messenger folded his hands behind his back to walk around him in a tight circle. "When you were taken up into the Doorway of Darkness—"

"You were there?"

"Let me finish."

Gabriel knew that tone. He put his teeth together.

"There were two options in that moment: extraction or retraction."

It was extraction, sadly.

"What you saw, your powers leaving, was what your powers needed you to see."

"It was an illusion?"

"Yes."

"I still have my powers?"

"No. Not like before."

Gabriel's heart ached. For a moment, he thought maybe, just maybe, he'd get them back.

"Your powers retreated inward because you, *Gabriel*, were dying. The only way to save you and themselves was to pull inward and preserve you." He paused and kept his circle. "In that world, you were exposed to something you were not equipped to face. Yes, you had been in that realm before long ago, but this time, you did not have the ability to withstand its sheer force. Your enemy created a door unlike its former, and he allowed it to not only just open, but interact with your world for a prolonged period of time. Interact with *you*." His voice grew a level louder and firmer. "Your teacher and Night Fowler were sent into the Doorway under my protection to retrieve you beneath Redsaw's notice. As far as was reported to me by your teacher, he thought the Doorway's realm consumed you, stole your power, and now . . ."

Gabriel's face grew hard. "What is he doing now?"

The messenger looked him in the eye, a gaze hidden behind bright light but one that sent a jolt through his soul all the same. "Reigning. Your world has become his.'"

It took him a moment to let it sink in. "And you let that happen?"

"Has your teacher taught you nothing?"

It seemed as if the messenger was going to say more but didn't. Gabriel kept silent.

"A merging of worlds is occurring now as we speak. As long as you have been away, that realm has yet to consume the entire planet."

"Then you have to stop him."

"He is not my agent to stop." The messenger put a hand on Gabriel's shoulder, sending a soothing electric warmth through him.

"I have so many questions," Gabriel said, tears pricking the corners of his eyes. "Valerie, me, Redsaw, you" —he nodded toward the dual doors— "them."

"In time," the messenger said. "And right now, time is not on our side." The messenger's hand never left his shoulder as the bright being rounded in front of him. The messenger put his other hand on Gabriel's other shoulder. "My son . . . close your eyes."

Gabriel did.

"What do you see?"

"Nothing. Just the inside of my eyelids. A bright, bloody red, the light—"

"No, Gabriel. What do you really see?"

He didn't know what the messenger meant.

"Look."

Gabriel searched the red murk that was his vision for any sign of—and there it was.

Bright blue crackles of energy sparked and burst within his closed eyes, a light shower of sparkling energy closing in from the sides and start to pop and burst before his vision.

"Now, my son," the messenger said, "receive your gift."

CHAPTER FIFTEEN

GABRIEL SLOWLY WALKED back to his quarters. He sensed outward, using his sphere. He was pretty sure the Central was completely empty except for him.

He opened the door but didn't turn on the light. Instead, he let the light from the hallway partially fill his room. His bed was mostly in shadow, but there was a lump on the mattress and it wasn't a bunched-up blanket.

Gabriel stepped over to his bed and slowly reached toward it. His fingers grazed the fabric. It was familiar yet foreign all the same. He grabbed a piece of it by the corner and drew the material closer to his eyes for a better look. He knew what this was.

He clenched the fabric in his fist then, a moment later, loosened his fingers, still holding it.

He looked the fabric over one more time. "This is different."

About the Author

A.P. Fuchs is the author of many novels and short stories. His most recent books are *Axiom-man/Crimson Cloak: Scarlet Synergy, Zomtropolis: A Record of Life in a Dead City,* and *Giganti-gator Death Machine: Triple Feature.*

Also a cartoonist, he is known for his superhero series, *The Axiom-man Saga*, both in novel and comic book format. Please visit **www.canisterx.com** for more on this series. For his webcomic, *Fredrikus*, about a down-and-out anthropomorphic dog in a dystopian sci-fi world, please go to **www.fredrikus.com**

As well, be sure to subscribe to A.P. Fuchs's YouTube Channel at **www.youtube.com/@apfuchs** for books, comics, podcasts, stories, and more.

www.ingramcontent.com/pod-product-compliance
Lightning Source LLC
Chambersburg PA
CBHW071020180726
48291CB00004B/1553